PRAISE FOR

The Bones We Haunt

"*THE BONES WE HAUNT* IS A LUSH, ROMANTIC, THOROUGHLY seductive Gothic Horror that stays with the reader long after the last line. Taylor expertly weaves rich prose, simmering dread, and beautiful atmosphere into a stunning tale of beastly desire and inner torture. Jane is a heroine the reader can so easily root for — plucky, curious, strange, and altogether delightfully endearing. This book is a must read for lovers of all things dark, delicious, and wolfy!" — Dorian Ravenscroft, author

"TAYLOR HAS CRAFTED A TRULY ONE-OF-A KIND WEREWOLF and romance story. Jane is such a fresh and compelling leading-lady, and the romance between her and Terence endeared and terrified me from its earliest drafts. Reading *THE BONES WE HAUNT* will not only excite and terrify you, but ask important questions about identity and societal/familial pressures. It does it all, delivering a heartfelt romance, heart-pounding horror, mystery and themes that will give you something to chew on long after reading." — Kaitlin Callahan, author and illustrator of "*The Farmer and The Wolf*"

JOSEPHINE TAYLOR

THE BONES WE HAUNT

First Edition: May 2025

Cover illustration and design by Erika Mariah Santos
Interior formatting and design by Mariska Maas (Rubre Art)

ISBN: 979-8-9926428-1-0 (Paperback)
ISBN: 979-8-9926428-0-3 (eBook)

Content Warnings

This following work contains graphic on-page depictions of gore, body horror, and peril; death of an animal (off page with on-page aftermath), death of a child (mentioned), poisoning of a child (mentioned), suicide (off page and mentioned), period-typical use of ableist language in referencing mental health, age gap relationship, use of a firearm, and allusions to Hell, demons, and occultism.

To Mom and Dad,
who still keep my dinosaur and
G3 My Little Pony figures in the same tote

Prologue

THE ONLY BARRIER BETWEEN THE BEAST'S TEETH AND the hunter's throat was the barrel of a Winchester Model 1895.

Mud surged around the hunter's shoulders, threatening to swallow him up as a great weight bore down on him. The taste of blood gushed across his tongue as he bit into his cheeks, his bottom lip, and he turned his head as the beast once more lunged forward with an audible snap of its jaws.

The hunter meant for this to be a swift kill, one done with a single shot. The sooner this hunt was over, the sooner he could revel in the guilt that would haunt him afterward. But the hesitation that caused his grip to shake and aim to lower resulted in the bullet lodging in the beast's shoulder, angering it instead of killing.

He barely had time to load another bullet before the beast burst from the fringes of the nearby forest—the glow of its yellow eyes and hunch of its back were unmistakable—and charged at him. Claws tore through mud, a maw was set on tasting vengeance.

It tackled him to the ground just as his thumb tapped the hammer. The force of monstrous paws suddenly upon his chest and the onslaught of rain from the heavens robbed him of his breath. The rifle was thrust upward to parry gnashing, starved teeth before they had a chance to taste his skin.

A full moon hung high above them, peering through the thick overcast to outline the beast in an unholy halo of light. Drool and blood leaked from its huffing mouth as teeth scraped against gunmetal and the hunter's raw knuckles.

Strength was beginning to bleed from the hunter's arms and he felt as though he were drowning, beneath the beast, mud, rain, and blood. It would be easy to let such happen: to forgo what had been requested of him to end this monster's misery. But the guilt of leaving a task incomplete and the guilt of committing murder were so similar that he couldn't decide which he'd rather live with.

His body seemingly made the decision for him when the muscles in his thighs bunched and he kicked until his boots met the beast's groin.

The beast choked on the air forced from its lungs with a choked squeal. It flinched back but failed to relent.

The hunter sucked in a breath the moment his cheeks no longer sweated beneath the blood-soaked stank of its breath and grunted as he heaved the beast back with another kick.

He didn't need an escape, he just needed enough space to pull that trigger...

The ground shuddered when the beast fell, showering the hunter in a spray of mud, blood, and rain.

Blood leaking from its shoulder, the beast wheezed. The vapor of its breath clouded its stained jaws and the bristle of its mane was made silver by the moon's waning light. Between its awful sounds, it let out what may have been a mewling whine. It was a sight equal parts pathetic and horrifying, though the hunter felt neither sympathy nor fear. Only the dread of duty.

The hunter raised the rifle until it nestled comfortably against his shoulder.

The beast whined as it looked at him with those sickly yellow eyes, and flashed its even yellower teeth. A challenge. A plea.

The hunter swallowed.

"I'm sorry, sir," he uttered—and pulled the trigger.

CHAPTER

One

14 NOVEMBER, 1905

T HE HOLLOW BELLY OF A WHALE GAPED DOWN AT JANE, yawning open like a maw of curved teeth.

The skeleton watched her closely with hollowed sockets, eyes that could no longer see, smelling her with nostrils that could no longer smell, and hungered with a belly that could no longer be starved. The preserved baleen's sleek, black bristles shone like obsidian beneath the sunlight that filtered through the museum's windows. A plaque told her that it was once a fin whale, whose body had washed up on a beach in Sussex, but to her, it was a monster, with its wide-open ribs waiting to gobble her up.

It both frightened and left her in awe knowing that such a creature swam the seas, and was *real*, was once alive, much like the skeletons of elephants and gorillas that occupied the museum in Milwaukee. To picture it being wrapped in the sarcophagus of blubbery flesh, stuffed with guts while pirouetting through the depths of the pitch-black ocean with an elegance that betrayed its awesome size made her lips tickle with a grin.

Jane had never been to Cambridge's University Museum of Zoology, but so far she was impressed by its rich collections, both anatomical and zoological. She struggled to decide if she favored this museum over London's Natural History Museum—though, to her, no collection could hold a candle to London's greater, grander specimen that was the whole *Diplodocus* skeleton. It was just back in May when she'd witnessed the ancient spectacle unveiled. An ancient creature resurrected to enamor modern eyes.

She wished she could've spent more time exploring this particular museum. She wanted to burrow and snoop through the whole extent of the collections stored in the depths of its belly, even if it did lack a whole dinosaur skeleton for her to fawn over. It certainly would've been far more exhilarating than sitting through another bore of a lecture.

She had once loved attending such lectures as a little girl. Seeing fossils displayed and discussed, reborn by academic mouths, she fooled herself into believing that her own interest in paleontology somehow made her an equal to those men. So much so that, more often than not, she allowed herself to be swept up in daydreams of standing upon those podiums, displaying whatever ancient bones she would have found in her pretend archeological digs in the garden or on the shores of the Great Lakes, shaped with arched horns and thousands of teeth like a dragon, to a gaslit theater of academics who would applaud her efforts.

Such interest waned as she matured and realized that such lectures were less of a celebration of enlightenment but rather a competition to see who had enough money to sound the most educated. It was why Jane was saddened that her father couldn't attend this particular series of lectures (which were about findings of the recent Saurian Expeditions in the States); she thought Dr. Simon Sterling was the only man ever of decent intelligence in a room.

At least none of these men were detonating each others' fossil finds—that Jane knew of. Though their war wasn't nearly as ruinous as the one waged between Edward Drinker Cope and Othniel Marsh (Jane would forever mourn any and all species lost in that Bone War, the ultimate fatalities), these academics still used bones and antiquity in an eternal act of posturing.

For a moment, Jane found a kinship in the assemblage of whale bones above her: suspended in time, forced to endure stuffy, academic competitions whilst yearning for freedom of the open ocean. Or, in Jane's circumstance, the freedom of the university's collections. Or a clothing shop, with her fingers plunged deep within the silken folds of a new gown.

"*Jane!*" A hand snatched Jane's elbow, startling her from her daydream.

Based on the intensity pinching the woman's mouth and punctuating her words, this wasn't her first attempt to get Jane's attention; Jane had been too enraptured with the whale skeleton to hear her mother's approach.

"They're gathering in the theater now, and I don't want to get poor seats again," Zelda Sterling—naturalist, artist, and ghostwriter for anyone who paid well enough—said with a firm grip.

By "poor seats," Mrs. Sterling meant the ones positioned toward the front of the theater, so close that they would have to crane their necks to look straight up at the podium. Those were the seats that the richest and oldest men scrambled to claim in their game of vying for the attention of whoever was speaking. If

Dr. Sterling was here, that's where he'd want to sit, or at the very least be forced to sit.

Everybody loved Dr. Simon Sterling and his lectures on paleobotany. Colleagues, professors, curators, and students alike were disheartened by the news that he couldn't be in attendance on account of contracting a horrid cold back home in the States and that they would have to contend with his wife and youngest daughter to attend in his stead.

How would they be able to wrestle with one another over who among them was his most devoted enthusiast when he wasn't present to hear their praises sweetened by milk and honey?

Jane had tried to ignore how when a man would greet her or her mother, he would look behind or around them in search for the beloved Dr. Sterling once he fulfilled the obligatory nicety of plastering on a too-polite grin for his too-polite greeting. She'd return it with her own vapid flashing of teeth. Couldn't they be satisfied enough having a conversation with only her?

What was wrong with a scientific conversation with a lady anyway? It wasn't Jane's fault that she had a tendency to detail the plum-colored ensemble and well-feathered merry widow hat she happened across in a shop window in the same breath as celebrating Lawrence Lambe's recent discovery of the *Centrosaurus* bones in Canada just last year.

Perhaps it was their own fault for being so disinterested in such colorful conversation. A theory Jane kept to herself was that the true reason as to why these men held so many degrees was to compensate for their lack of knowledge regarding the proclivities of the female sex.

Mrs. Sterling took Jane by the elbow and together they followed the trickling of men in suits and their wives in shapely gowns to the museum's main theater. There weren't many that

Jane recognized among all these most-likely-Cambridge-doctors, at least well-enough to strike up easy small talk, so she kept close to her mother. She did catch some glancing at her dress, however, which was a loud shade of pink with ruffled white lace bunched around her bodice and the opal charm clasped upon her throat, and she smirked, not hesitating in adding a flaunting flow to her stride so that the lace and fine fabric caught prettily in the sunlight. If others didn't wish to converse with her, then the least they could do was spare her wardrobe an envious look.

From the flowing crowd, a short, stocky man with snow-white mutton chops broke away to walk toward the Sterlings. He was smiling, with his wife at his elbow.

Jane studied the woman's pale gray dress with a raised brow. The puffed sleeves and stiff bodice recalled images of silhouettes of the previous decade, and Jane speculated that she had nothing newer in her wardrobe to wear. The ensemble was completed by a modest green hat, parasol, and emerald-jeweled choker. Jane cringed, though affectionately, as she had begrudgingly accepted that Mrs. Elizabeth Talbot wasn't savvy with what was presently fashionable. It was all tacky, to Jane, but there was some character in tackiness.

"Oh, Zelda, Mary! How lovely to see you again!" The man said, his tone bright and aged—and American. His wife smiled as well, nodding her greeting. She was similar to her husband: white-haired, wrinkled, and stocky in build.

Jane winced at the use of her nickname, "Mary." It was an alias she crafted as a child, when her paleontological aspirations were big and thriving, but had long since outgrown. She smiled, nonetheless.

"Mr. Talbot, Elizabeth, hello!" Mrs. Sterling greeted them with a warm grin. Her hands, outstretched, found those of Mrs. Talbot's. The cloth of her gloves strained as she imprinted her affections into her old friend's skin. "It's been far too long."

Jane inclined her head in a nod that displayed the details of tinseled feathers and silk roses sewn into her hat when the Talbots offered her their quieter greetings. She last met them at the unveiling of the *Diplodocus* exhibit in London. The Talbots weren't necessarily scientists, neither of them holding degrees or possessing any tangible education in the sciences to boast about, but rather passionate patrons of the Smithsonian in Washington.

About once a year, in the late spring when the Sterlings would take holiday in Saratoga Springs, the Sterlings and the Talbots would share a suite for the month-long duration of their stays, and in such a way a bond like that of family had been forged between them. In a way, Jane nearly considered the Talbots as surrogate grandparents, as she didn't have any more living ones with whom she shared blood and bone.

"Yes, I agree," Mrs. Talbot said as she took a moment to cup Jane's chin before returning her attention to Mrs. Sterling.

Jane caught Mr. Talbot looking around, looking over Mrs. Sterling's shoulders, and she resisted the urge to roll her eyes.

The number of chins Mr. Talbot possessed doubled as he skewered his lips into an exaggerated frown. It was an expression that would have had Jane in a fit of giggles as a child, but now only a huff of amusement rushed from her nostrils. "I see no sign of Simon. Will he not be present?"

"No, no," Mrs. Sterling pursed her lips. "He's ill with an infection, I'm afraid."

Mrs. Talbot pressed a hand to her chest with a low *tsk*. "Oh, how dreadful."

Mr. Talbot smoothed blunt fingers over his bristly, white mustache. "Yes, that is very unfortunate."

Mrs. Sterling took both of Mrs. Talbot's hands and worried her mouth into a pursed line, as if on the verge of tears. Very clearly a mask, one anyone could see as a dramatic ruse, as Dr. Sterling's "infection" was nothing more than a mere head cold that only brought him mild discomfort and exhaustion. Mrs. Sterling and Jane were alike in that way: stretching the truth just enough to warrant extra attention, but not pity. It seemed to have worked, as Mrs. Talbot stepped closer to her friend with coos of reassurances and well-wishes rushing from her mouth.

As Mrs. Sterling and the Talbots spoke, Jane stood off to the side, listening, smiling, nodding, and laughing whenever the conversation required it. But it didn't take long for her to grow tired of the same "how are you"s and "what have you been doing"s that were shared whenever they reunited with the Talbots. There was only so much small talk between those who have known each other for decades—and have lived stagnant lives for twice as long—a woman of twenty-four could handle, so she allowed her eyes to wander the room.

Repeatedly her attention was drawn away from the crowd of puff-sleeved bodices, slim skirts, and plainly-colored ditto suits and back toward the fin whale suspended high above, haloed by sunlight and an arched ceiling. It continued to watch her as though it were a predator tempting her back to it with its magnificence. Its gaping ribs were poised to swallow a man standing in its shadow, just as she had been doing moments ago. Even from behind Jane recognized the man's slumped shoulders, so she kept her steps as quiet as possible as she parted from her companions to approach him.

Excitement made her final few steps clack sharply against the marble floor before she pounced on the man, and roared, "*A-hah*! A new victim to be gobbled up by the big bad whale!"

The two of them cried: her from thrill, him from terror.

It felt as though the world paused as the ambiance of studious conversation hushed into leering silence, and several heads turned to look their way.

Jane supposed that she should have been embarrassed, but she was too focused on trying to breathe amidst her pealing laughter as the man reached for his chest to settle his beating heart.

She at last regained just enough breath to say, "My word, is that Mr. Terence Hayes I see? In the flesh? Or are you just an apparition?" She pinched his arm to assure herself of his corporeality.

The man was tall and broad-shouldered, though not in the sense that his size was monstrous or athletic. More like a wall of stone, a barrier of flesh and bone determined to protect and defend. Much like a great wall, he always seemed weathered to Jane, even though he couldn't have been older than forty, with threads of silver at the temples of his otherwise dark, neatly-groomed hair and the bruised flesh around his eyes. His clean-shaven face was long, hollow, and sagging from what seemed to be perpetual exhaustion, but he always held a quiet politeness in his hazel-brown eyes that Jane had been drawn to since they first met. It was a visage she likened to a lazing basset hound, and she grinned as a warm sensation blossomed in her chest when he looked at her.

"Miss Sterling, you startled me," Terence Hayes released a ragged breath but quickly composed himself. A hand smoothed the front of his purple waistcoat.

No, not purple, Jane noted. *Mauve.*

He cleared his throat. "Yes, yes, it is me, in the flesh, you are not mistaken. How have you been? It feels as though it has been half an age since we last met."

"Well enough. Though, I'd rather not be stuck going to a lecture on a Saturday afternoon, not with the weather being as fine as it is," Jane whined, pouting her lips as she gazed longingly out the windows and at a courtyard painted by the rare golden hues by the oncoming autumn sunset. "I'd forgotten how gloomy your England can be. I was hoping to cherish the sun before it decided to vanish again!"

"It *is* autumn, Miss Sterling," his gaze dropped to her dress, a thick brow raised. "You seem to be properly dressed for the weather with all those layers."

Jane clicked her tongue and rolled her eyes. "It only *looks* layered because of the lace. See?" She toyed with the pleated fringes of her dress, displaying the white lace decorating the bulk of her pink skirts. Ruffles of the glittering lace fringed from the puffed fabric of her shoulders and pillowed around the cuffs of her silken sleeves, which she held out for him to inspect closer. "Just lace."

"Ah, my mistake," he said in a voice that rumbled gently from his chest, reaching her ears with a tender caress. He leaned close, eyes narrowed, to better observe her ensemble; a heavy scent of bergamot and damp earth washed over her. "Quite well-made, Miss Sterling. It's attractive on you."

Jane couldn't resist another grin, though she was unsure if it was inspired by smug satisfaction or the heated fluttering in her chest. This gown was one she requested specifically for this trip. While her father's pocketbook refused her the chance to purchase a thing directly from Paris, she was able to convince the Sterlings' favored dressmaker Mrs. Robinson to craft an exact replica of the blossom-pink dress Jane had glimpsed in an issue of *La Mode Illustrée*. Years of patronage from the Sterlings, an invite to afternoon tea, and a handsome sum of $30 were all the costs it took for the old seamstress to agree to the sudden commission. And Jane was excited that such an impulsive request was yielding the desired results. Though Terence Hayes was just one person, to dazzle one man was enough to dazzle a crowd.

Jane's poise faltered slightly before burgeoning once more

when Terence took her outstretched hand and brought it to his lips so they may bump against her gloved knuckles—the whisper of what *might* have been a kiss. His hands trembled, but this tremor was something he'd always possessed, as far as Jane could remember from when she'd first met him at the exhibition in May. She'd rued that their meeting had been so brief, underneath the *Diplodocus* skeleton, not too unlike the scene they engaged with now, as he had been in a rush to catch an afternoon train from London to Cambridge.

"It's a pleasant surprise to see you again, Miss Sterling," the confidence that glimmered in Jane's chest dimmed when he started to look behind her—searching. "I heard that your father will be in attendance. Will he be joining us?"

Jane wasn't afraid to let her disappointment show, propping a hand upon her hip and letting her smile fall into an unsatisfied curl of her lip. "No, he will not—"

"Oh, Mr. Hayes, hello!" Mrs. Sterling appeared at Jane's side and took hold of her elbow. Her brow pinched, and her smile softened, as she reached forward and squeezed his arm, a gesture of sympathy. "I hope you have been doing well, dear boy. I am terribly sorry to hear about your brother. A good man, he was."

Jane's blood chilled and her cheeks flushed. She'd forgotten the news she heard of the late Matthew Hayes's passing. She knew very little of his death aside from a rumor her mother shared with her over breakfast as they were still crossing the Atlantic, that he had been shot in a hunting accident a month ago. Though the ghastliness of such a whisper was enough for her to keep it at the back of her mind out of intrigue, she had otherwise forgotten about it as she didn't anticipate seeing Terence in attendance today, nor did he wear any tokens of mourning. She was unprepared to offer condolences.

Guilt smacked her across the cheek with an ice-cold hand, and she withheld a grimace as she lowered her head and took a step back, allowing her mother more space to comfort.

"Yes, yes, thank you. A good man he was indeed," Terence said quickly, clearing his throat in a manner hinting at a mounting discomfort. His smile was tight, brief, a polite obligation. "Will Dr. Sterling be joining us?"

Mrs. Sterling's expression started to morph into her trademark pout. "Oh, no, I'm afraid he won't be. Too ill to travel—only the flu, bless him, but he didn't think he could survive on a boat with his condition."

Heat flooded Jane's chest once more as Terence inclined his head. "My deepest apologies, Sterlings, I hope that his recovery is swift. Do send him my condolences that he couldn't be with us today, will you?"

There was always something so attractive about a man who allowed himself to display a genuine concern.

"I will. He regrets being unable to attend," Mrs. Sterling placed a hand atop her breast. "It breaks his weary heart when he misses these lectures."

"Such a shame... I had been eager to speak with him regarding a proposition. It seems that you will also have to tell him that I send him my heartfelt greetings," Terence said, hands clasped behind his back.

Mrs. Sterling touched his shoulder in the feminine mimicry of a mate clapping a hand there. "But of course! He's spoken so fondly of you since his London trip, and I must admit we were rather impressed by the collection of *gryphaea* specimens you sent home with him. I think they're still displayed in his study cabinet. He'd be thrilled to know you said hello!"

Terence nodded curtly again, his smile tight but not unfriendly. It at least reached his eyes—Jane liked it when men smiled with their eyes, more so than with their teeth. "I only regret not bringing with me more specimens so that you may bring them home to him as a souvenir."

Behind them, there was a gentle murmur that had been dying to a dull whisper as the last of the crowd filed into the theater.

"I suppose we ought to go find ourselves seats, yes?" Terence gestured for Jane and Mrs. Sterling to lead as they made their way to the stuffy theater. Jane kept her steps short so she could walk a little closer to him.

The theater was a wide and dim lecture hall, with a single stage at the room's very front illuminated by gaslight, framed by blank chalkboards, and surrounded by an army of cushioned seats, most of which were already occupied. The only vacant seats available were at the very back of the room, steeped in shadows.

Jane turned to Terence, looking up at him. The dark lighting made his eyes molasses-brown.

"Sit with us, won't you?" She took his arm and lightly tugged, not at all intent on releasing him. She leaned closer to whisper, "I predict that this will be *awfully* dull, and I'd appreciate having someone to share comments with—otherwise I'm *certain* I'll die of boredom!" She pulled on him again, pouted her pink lips, and fluttered her lashes in heavy, sad blinks. "*Please*, Mr. Hayes?"

He was hot beneath her touch, even through the layers of his suit and her gloves. His eyes fluttered with their own frantic blinks as he licked his lips. Was he blushing or was that just low light playing on his cheeks? He cleared his throat.

"It'd be a delight, Miss Sterling. I certainly wouldn't wish for you to die—under any circumstances—but boredom would be quite an unsightly way to go," he whispered with words that held a muted smile to them and followed Jane to a trio of open seats where she sat comfortably between him and Mrs. Sterling.

Not even a heartbeat passed before a short man with a finely groomed silver beard stepped up to the podium and announced his presence with an obnoxious, wet clearing of his throat. The moment Jane recognized him as Dr. Charles Greene, a fellow paleobotanist her father described as being 'amateur' for letting his heart become ensnared within a cage of industry and empire forged by discovery rather than for the wonder such science could nurture, she decided to pay him no mind as he began to speak. She let the world around her to fall silent as she eased into the numbness of quietly existing.

She continued to half-listen, only offering applause whenever anyone else did between speakers. It turns out they were arguing—well, arguing in the sense that each man who spoke after Dr. Greene would attempt to discredit the previous man's statement with progressively petty remarks veiled behind the sophistication of scientific vernaculars and European accents—about the identity of a new kind of fossilized fern from the Saurian Expedition in Nevada. Or perhaps they were speaking about *Ichthyosaur* skeletons found on the same expedition. Jane couldn't bring herself to care enough to pay proper attention. It all came to sound like the cacophony of dogs snapping, albeit politely, at each other's throats for a scrap of bone.

Instead, she busied herself with scribbling on a museum brochure with one of the charcoal pencils hidden in the depths of her mother's purse. And on the pamphlet she drew beasts. Winged ones with beaks filled with jagged teeth. Some of them were chewing the heads off of stick-figure caricatures with beards and monocles. She felt Terence's observing stare, felt him lean close ever so slightly, so she shifted her hand as she pretended to sit back and examine her work, allowing him a peek.

"What are these meant to be?" He whispered, a low, rumbling sound in the dark.

"*Pterosaurs*, obviously! Can't you see the wings?" Jane traced over the multitude of wings with the pencil.

"Ah, yes, I suppose I do see it now," he hummed, his breath tousling a strand of her hair. "My mistake, Miss Sterling. I must say, the teeth and whiskers are a creative detail."

The lecture continued, about what Jane no longer knew as her mind had begun to wander once more, and she had grown curious as to why Terence would have been in attendance. As far as she was aware, he, like the Talbots, was not a man of science and attended such lectures because he had the interest and free time. He never seemed too inclined to speak with other doctors and scientists, so she wondered what had made her father so special that an English gentleman would be seeking his company.

She resumed her sketching, this time drawing a triceratops with arcing horns and hunched back like that of a charging bison, and when there was an eruption of applause following another speaker, she asked, "So, what business do you have with my father?"

Leaning closer to exchange his own whisper, Terence said, "I've recently found fossils in my garden. Ones of old plants, it seems, that I cannot recognize, so I felt it a stroke of luck when I heard your father would be in attendance today. It's a shame he isn't here, but I can always send him correspondence of what I found, and donate them to the museum regardless. I would've liked to have known what they are, to know their worth. I'm not sharp enough to be versed in paleobotany, unfortunately, so I don't trust myself to properly identify them."

Jane raised a brow. "What's stopping you from asking Dr. Greene for assistance?" She used her charcoal pencil to gesture to said professor from where he had long since fallen asleep in his seat, head resting back and his mouth hanging agape. If it weren't for the snores rattling in his throat, she would have thought that he was dead.

"Your father is a rare breed of man. His studies are his passion and not a tool in a competition. And I find him considerably more approachable. Dr. Greene, I fear, would find my request too trivial and meager," Terence hummed and rested his chin upon a knuckle, then nodded toward the other end of the room, to an elderly man with a back so crooked Jane thought he resembled a question mark. Doctor Alan Thaddeus Hawthorne—the Second, Jane reminded herself—a professor of botany from London, though it seemed as though he looked more like he were pulled from a crypt rather than a university hall.

"Should I also refrain from asking for Dr. Hawthorne's opinion?" Terence smirked with muted humor.

Jane clicked her tongue and flashed her teeth before resuming her sketching. "He may be a safe bet. He has a deeply... intimate knowledge of paleontology, you know?"

Something genuine passed behind Terence's eyes, stifling their brief flicker of mischief. He looked at the old doctor again in reassessment. "Is that so?"

She nodded, biting her lip against a smirk. "Well, I'd sure hope so, given he looks as though he's peeped up his fair share of dinosaur dames' skirts before inviting them to a waltz in bed." She didn't wait for his response before stifling a cackle behind her hand, failing to capture her snort. The sound echoed in the theater and she heard the creak of chairs as many eyes turned to stare.

It wasn't until Jane felt Mrs. Sterling pinch her arm and seethe a sharp "*Janet!*" in her ear that she finally tamed herself into silence. She nearly fell into hysterics once more when she braved a glance in Terence's direction and saw a ruddy blush on his cheeks.

Mrs. Sterling's fingers remained curled and poised to pinch again for the remainder of the lecture. Whenever Jane caught mother's glare in her periphery, bravery threatened to curdle into foolishness, and she pressed her lips into a tightened line in an attempt to keep laughter contained deep between her ribs.

Such behavior persisted until the lecture ended with another series of applause. Neither the Sterlings nor Terence rose from their seats until Dr. Hawthorne passed by in his hobbling departure, which was when Jane and Terence exchanged a knowing look. His cheeks burned pink and Jane snorted—again—as they left the theater.

Once they were back in the main hall, Terence cleared his throat and situated his hands behind his back. "Well, missus and ma'am," he nodded to both Jane and Mrs. Sterling respectively, "It's been lovely to see you both again. How long will you be in Cambridge?" He lingered on Jane for a heartbeat too long before scratching at his cheek, itching away any blush that might have remained there.

"Until the end of the month," Mrs. Sterling answered. "We booked the suite until the end of November, and... well, *I* would hate to waste the weeks we have left."

"Then I would be delighted to offer you ladies a tour of the city," he said quickly. "There is much to see here, and I'd be heartbroken if you dared to return to America disappointed in what you've seen."

"And we would be delighted by your company," Mrs. Sterling said with a shrill coo as she touched his arm. "Our suite is at the University Arms. You're always a guest with us, Mr. Hayes. Let us plan for an outing soon—tomorrow morning, perhaps?"

"I don't see why not tomorrow. Expect me there in the morning, then, where I shall bid you both a warm welcome to the city, and perhaps a luncheon," he smiled then, and his gaze lingered on Jane once more.

"I think it could be fun," Jane offered. She smudged her gloves with charcoal marks as she worried the pamphlet between her fingers. "But! Come no earlier than nine! Dear Mama will need all the time she can get to put on her face."

Mrs. Sterling cleared her throat, "Are we sure it's *me* who will require an eon, and then some, for putting on face?"

Jane's cheeks heated as she balked at her mother. She couldn't deny the truth behind her words, but did she need to say them in front of Terence?

Her embarrassment fizzled away, though only slightly, upon hearing his rumbling laugh.

"Let us settle for nine-thirty, then, ladies. Take all the time that you will require for putting on your faces," he said and offered Jane a small smirk. "But until then—I bid you ladies a good day."

He took turns shaking each of their hands with a gentle grip as a final farewell before making his departure. He caged Jane's hand a heartbeat longer than he did Mrs. Sterling's, and Jane was certain the brush of his thumb across her knuckles was to ensure the kiss he left there before would remain stamped into her skin.

"Until tomorrow, Miss Sterling," he whispered to her, and her only, before letting go. He held her stare until finally looking down at the shined shoes that he pivoted, and turned.

Jane trained her eyes on the center of his broad back as he walked away, melting into the gilded crowd like a shadow, and shivered at the sudden flicker of excitement in her belly. She squeezed the pamphlet tighter this time, so that she may capture the lingering heat from his touch for a moment longer.

CHAPTER

Two

ANE AWOKE TO THE WARMTH OF SUNLIGHT FILTERING through the windows, washing the room in beams of pure gold. She stretched in the morning heat, sprawling her limbs across the cream-colored sheets, or at least as much as she could without disrupting her mother sleeping right beside her. When they first arrived at the University Arms, the only suites available were ones with a single bed, which would have been perfect if it were still only Dr. and Mrs. Sterling as initially planned, but Jane didn't mind. She was always too tired at the end of the night to really care if she shared a bed, and she wouldn't complain about the extra heat. It filled in the void on a mattress that would otherwise be occupied by Mr. Thompson at home, with his twitching whiskers and thumbed paws.

She rose from the bed, draped herself in a robe, and tip-toed into the suite's parlor room to phone down to the concierge to have coffee brought up; her shadow cast on the opposing wall reminded her of a hedgehog, with her short hair tousled to jut out every which way.

Her feet absorbed the heat of the hardwood floor she crossed to look out one of the two bay windows in the room and watched Cambridge come to life. To her, it wasn't too unlike the view her bedroom offered of Milwaukee. She looked upon choked streets and bustling sidewalks that achingly reminded her of home. Her eyes tracked the sweeping of skirts over the brick road, the skipping of boots as they evaded the clop of hooves and scrape of carriage wheels, and with a sigh she pressed her cheek against the window. The glass had a chill to it, seeping deep into her skin and fogging beneath her breath. She smudged away the condensation by tracing loose, swirling patterns with the tip of a pinky finger.

She jumped at a knocking at the suite door. Panic flickered between her breasts for a moment, fearing that Terence had arrived early, but calmed herself when she opened the door to the concierge with a tray of French press. After paying the boy a tip, she was alone again.

She drank coffee at the window, smudged with the echoes of her swirling fingertips, as she schemed what outfit she'd wear for the day out. She'd dress loudly, of course. She wanted people to see her, she wanted Terence to remember time spent with her if not for her eccentricities then for her ostentatious wardrobe. Rarely did she have a chance to impress a man on her own terms (let alone one she was fond of) before her sisters would swoop in to snatch him up with their lyrical seductions, leaving Jane to stumble over fossil trivia in their wake. Terence's attention would be all hers this time, her sisters and their songs far away on a different continent.

Her hands started to shake, though she couldn't determine

whether it was from the coffee or her excitement—or perhaps it was a bit of both. With a small hum, she left her coffee on the window sill and set to work.

From her trunk, she pulled free a dress a shocking shade of chartreuse, with fabric that shone like freshly shined metal, notably in the puffed sleeves that tapered into tight cuffs at the wrists; the glass pearls sewn into the high collar, sleeves, and bodice gave the dress even more of shimmer as Jane slipped into it. It wasn't quite the shade of those arsenic-laced gowns from yesteryear, but rather like that of a secluded glade illuminated by midmorning sunlight. It was a similar color to Jane's own eyes, downturned, heavy-lidded, and set a tad too far apart from one another, though she always disliked their stony-green hue. If it were up to her, she'd prefer brown, or even black—a color that could be versatile with any ensemble. Green eyes were too striking and demanding of attention. But Jane found ways to make do, namely by using a dark brown pencil to smudge and darken around her eyes.

In the parlor's long mirror, she admired herself, twirling to see how sunlight danced across its skirt. A part of her hoped Terence would equal parts admire it and find it exasperating, whatever it took for the image of her to be forever imprinted into his psyche and claimed as her own.

However, what she hoped would truly capture his attention was her hair as she started to tame it with the assistance of a rose oil tincture and boar bristle brush. It was shorn short in a masculine cut, barely long enough to even curl her dark-colored bangs with a pair of heating tongs. And she liked it that way. There was less for her to fuss with and it also earned her attention. When she wore no hat or veil, her hair never went unnoticed. And she reveled in it. It could've been a curious stare, one of disdain, judgment, or disgrace, she didn't care all that much. As long as she could flaunt it and people saw her, then their disapproval was worth it.

The character of her voice was similar: nasal and abrasive, with an emphasis on vowels in the back of her throat, so that it may be heard from all corners of a room. She first developed the inflection as a teenager, when she'd finally acquired an eye for fashion and the desire to be noticed from within the shadows of her sisters' achievements germinated into a wretched blossom. It remained that way as she entered womanhood, and no longer could she remember what her voice ought to have sounded like, much like how she'd forgotten what her hair would be like if it hung at a long and proper length.

To complete her ensemble, Jane wore a new set of pearl earrings, gloves, a parasol, and a locket hanging above her collarbone.

Returning to the mirror, she lightly fingered the charm—a trilobite fossil preserved in resin so that nothing may harm it. It was her first fossil, found on the shores of Lake Michigan. She was three or four, an age she couldn't exactly place, when she'd accompanied her father on a casual walk, as she had always done. Her little paw was captured in his hand that guided her as her gaze remained fixated solely on the pebbles that shifted beneath her bare feet. She'd nearly tripped when she found a gray pebble with an oblong blot of brown in its center, and even to this day she vividly recalled the way Dr. Sterling's eyes shone as she held up the stone.

"*Calymene celebra*," he explained to her whilst coaxing her little thumb along the crustaceous exoskeleton. "A trilobite, Janie. This whole state used to be drowned in water, once upon a time, in an era before mammoths and ice shelves."

At the time, Jane had been both enthralled and terrified by the prospect of her home being drowned in prehistoric water. Although, the dreams she had of trilobites and deiphons and mammoths walking the streets of Milwaukee in waistcoats whilst waiting for trams had eased her fear enough to instead reconstruct it into wonder.

The little stone had been with her ever since.

A knock at the door took her attention away from the mirror. The same concierge that brought her coffee stood on the threshold with Terence looming behind him when she opened the door.

"Mr. Hayes, miss," the boy nodded, then was gone, leaving Jane and Terence alone in the entryway.

Jane stepped aside and beckoned for Terence to enter. "Well, don't be a stranger, Mr. Hayes. There's still coffee left if you would like a cup," she said, but her offer was met with silence. He was staring at her hair, and she smirked as she tucked a short, curled strand behind her ear. "Do you like it?"

"Are you ill?" he asked in a low, considerate whisper. He worried the brim of a tophat between quivering fingers. His question was thick in what it asked.

"Ill" meant many things concerning womanhood. He may as well have asked if she had once been thrown in a madhouse or a sanatorium, had sold her hair, or was riddled with mites all in three simple words. The question itself hadn't bothered Jane, having been asked it by family when she first cut her hair, it was the fact that Terence was the one to have asked it.

She refused to let it toy with her morale and she maintained a toothy smile.

"Not at all. Can you imagine having hair that hung almost to the floor, how long it takes to groom?" she asked, raising a brow and settling a hand upon her hip.

He winced as if taking the time to imagine such a scenario. "I suppose you're right, Miss. Sterling. But... you *are* all right, yes?"

She lightly patted his arm at that. "Very much so. Quite excited for our little outing!"

His shoulders seemed to relax a bit and a breath rushed from his nose in a sigh. "Oh, delightful, then." He looked into the suite behind her. "Will Mrs. Sterling be joining us?"

"No, I don't believe so," Jane tried to make such words come across with little enthusiasm as she puckered her lips into a pout. If she were to at last be free of her sisters' influence, so, too, did she wish to be free of her mother's. She didn't require a chaperone! "A lady needs her beauty sleep, and you should know that my mother isn't a woman to give up the chance for beauty sleep!"

He chuckled and smiled in a way that deepened the shallow wrinkles lining his eyes. "I suppose you're right. Well, I won't be the poor soul to dare disturb a lady's slumber. It's a shame she won't be able to come along, but I suppose there will be time for future luncheons during your ladies' stay. Shall we begin our excursion, then, Miss Sterling?"

Yes! Her heart sang, and she hurried to retrieve her hat, parasol, and coat.

"And, Terence, please—" she started as she fumbled with her coat. He perked at the sound of her voice, like a dog after its name had been called. "Just call me 'Jane.'"

† †† ╷† † ╽†╷† † ╷ ††

"Anyplace you wish to see first?" Terence asked as they stepped outside and up to an awaiting cab. Beside it was a man younger than Jane, thin and boyish, fair-haired, and wearing working clothes underneath an overcoat.

The boy gave Jane a curt nod and tight-lipped smile. His narrow chin was patched with pale stubble. He was stroking the muzzle of the sturdy white mare pulling the cab. Along his bony jawline, Jane noticed faded bruises, brown and jaundiced with healing.

Jane returned the gesture, and answered for Terence, "I know not a single thing about this city. I am a stranger here, a puppet, and I permit you to become my puppet master, Mr. Hayes." She held her arms up and offered them limply to him as if he was indeed in possession of those marionette strings.

"Wonderful, then." His grin was wide enough that she caught a flash of his front teeth that crossed over one another ever so slightly, a pinch of his eyes, an assured arch of his brows as he opened the door for her. He offered her his hand, which she used to hoist herself into the velvet-lined box.

Is that what confidence looks like on his face? She thought with a tingling heat at the tips of her ears. *He should wear it more often—it makes him quite handsome.*

"Take us to the university gardens, please, Ruben," he said to the boy whilst giving him a good clap on the arm, as though he were speaking to a brother or son, then joined her in the carriage.

"Oh, university gardens?" Jane breathed. Then paused. "But it's November. Surely such gardens would be spent by now."

"Thank God for greenhouses, I say," he said from where he sat across from her. He braced himself, allowing her space, as the cab lurched forward. "And pardon for neglecting to say so sooner, but your dress is lovely, Jane. I quite like the pearls."

† †† ¡† † ͰͰͺͲ † ͳ † ͳ ₊†₊

JUST AS JANE ANTICIPATED, THE GARDENS WERE GRAY AND brown. The grass possessed the faintest sheen of the morning's frost melting beneath the sunlight. Unfortunately, the moment she and Terence stepped from the cab, the sun had become muted, hiding under the thin coverage of clouds that threatened afternoon rain.

Other people visiting the garden were as drab as the gardens themselves, wrapped in bleak hues that Jane sniffed at. Terence himself dressed in all gray and purple, like a bruise. It made Jane's dress all the greener, and she held herself a little higher as she adjusted her hat.

Although she couldn't deny the practicality of their clothes, layered in coats and cloaks, must they wear their garments so shoddily? She shivered and nuzzled her nose into the mink-fur collar of the pink coat that matched the color of her gloves, her lips. At least *she* could balance an act of utility and flair.

When Terence offered her his elbow, she took it with a grateful sigh and practically hugged his arm as a way to absorb his warmth.

He led her across the chilled lawn, past half-shriveled plants, and greenery that tried desperately to cling to their last living leaves, branches, and flowers before the autumn air took them. Trees that circled the lawn wore seasonal orange-brown leaves, but they weren't beautiful, at least not to Jane. To her, the trees just looked *dead*. A light gust of air sighed across the lawn, disrupting the leaves, and prompting Jane to press into Terence with a shiver.

Terence cleared his throat as he tensed beneath her. His usual tremor remained.

"Are trees like this at this time of year in America?" he asked, and Jane thought it would've been condescending if it were coming from a different mouth, but he seemed to have been asking out of a genuine curiosity—and also an eagerness to fill silence with conversation. "Forgive me for asking something so simple. It's just I've never traveled across the pond, so I wouldn't know."

Jane shook her head. "These trees are so... sad." She didn't hold back a disappointed sneer. She lightly scuffed at the ground with the end of her parasol. "It's nothing like in America. I live along the Great Lakes, and the trees there are just... Well, they're *wonderful.* You go to the north, toward Canada, and the maples shine gold and bleed sweetness." She recalled images of the labyrinthine tanglings of tubing often strung, with the intricacy of a spider's web, between the towering monoliths that were gilded northwood maples as they collected that coveted syrup. Did they have anything like that in England? "And you're never quite as alone as you'd think, y'know, in the woods. There is always the company of foxes and bears and deer and squirrels, and so, so many lakes that reflect foliage like a mirror—oh, you would *love* it, Terence! And I mustn't leave out the blue jays. They scream and scream, but I cannot help but love them. They're the anthem of autumn, you know."

"Hmm…" Slowly, he nodded, licking his lips with a savoring sigh, as if he were desperately trying to experience the foreign memory for himself. When his eyes met hers, they held the deference of a dog tethered to its kennel, never meant to experience such awe for itself, and having long since been submissive to that fact. "Yes… Yes, I think I would rather like that. I'd like that very much, Miss Sterl—*Jane.*"

Jane mustered a grin to combat the rising sadness his gaze suddenly inflicted upon her. She dug her fingers into him as she let him continue guiding her to the large greenhouse at the edge of the circular lawn.

The greenhouse was a castle of glass and iron. It was a single-story structure, wide and squat and ornate, with white metal framework that arched like a fin whale's rib. A creature in its own right.

It was considerably warmer inside, enough so that Jane detached herself from Terence's side to wander along the gravel path. She paused before a patch of ferns, a frond reaching out with a natural elegance to kiss at her skirts. She rifled around in her purse until she found her spectacles, and, keeping them folded, brought them up to her face just enough so she could read the plaque.

"*Athyrium filix-femina,*" she hummed aloud, hoping that it made her sound smart.

"Lady fern," Terence mumbled beside her, hands held behind his back. He nodded to her glasses. "Bad eyes?"

"Only when reading," she said and hastily put them back in her purse. As she never seemed to find a way to properly accessorize glasses, she'd never been fond of them, utilizing them as little as possible. And, as petty as it was, she never viewed glasses as attractive—on any sex, but especially not on her. Clearing her throat, she gestured to the plants. "Fond of plants, are you?"

He shook his head, then lightly tapped at the plaque again, where both the fern's scientific and common names were placed. "Merely observant."

"Oh," Jane blushed.

He winked with a hint of a smirk. "But I suppose I find their quiet company comfortable, on occasion. Ruben is the one who takes a liking to plants and animals. I prefer to think of myself as a naturalist—by hobby, of course—not a gardener."

She opened her mouth to speak but shut it with an audible clack of her teeth as a flash of color flitted through her vision, followed by the tickle of legs against her cheek. She gasped and held her breath, going still as she withered beneath the butterfly's mercy. The daughter of a botanist—or, well, *paleo*botanist—she may be, but a friend of insects she was not.

"Oh, my. It seems as though we have a guest," Terence's chest rumbled with a chuckle. "Allow me, Jane…"

He reached forward and coaxed the butterfly onto his finger. His touch lingered upon her cheek, and it burned. Even through his gloves, Jane felt as though she were being branded—and it was exquisite. His dark hazel eyes bore into her, and hers into him, holding each other captive within unseen cages. Everything burned, pleasantly.

Her heart stuttered in her throat. She suddenly hungered for more of his whispering, heated touches and fervid stares.

Was the heat always this overwhelming? Or was that just the greenhouse's natural humidity?

The butterfly twitched its wings of iridescent emerald and black upon his knuckle still caressing her cheek.

"*Graphium agamemnon*—the tailed jay," Jane whispered at last, breathless. She wasn't fond of bugs, but she liked to know the names of pretty things—and this just so happened to be one of several species of butterflies her mother had pinned in her studio.

His mouth eased into a gentle slope of a smile. "Fascinating," he murmured with that rolling purr that found a way to comfort her very bones.

Just as she was becoming addicted to his touch, Jane tore her gaze away with a clearing of her throat. Startled, the butterfly shuttered upwards into the greenhouse's glass heavens.

"I-If you're no true naturalist, it makes me curious as to why you would bring me here." *I would much rather return to the museum*, she thought and hoped he could somehow hear it. It took every bit of her willpower to not raise her hand and cup where he held her face, to savor the heat that haunted the flesh there.

The confidence that'd previously charmed his features crumbled as his brows knit together.

"I-I thought it would've made for a nice scenic walk given the time of year. Forgive me, I've always found these gardens to be rather calming—" His words stumbled and slurred, and Jane couldn't resist a small laugh. She made him nervous. She liked that. She could hold influence over a nervous man—just what she required to recover from... whatever influence he had over *her*.

"Not that I mind," she said with a shrug and latched back onto his arm, like a parasite clinging to the tongue of a fish, leeching off his warmth. "I trust you know where you lead me."

His tremoring paused, and his hand clasped atop hers. "I... appreciate that, Jane..."

† †† ı† † ˥† ı† † ˥ı †† ˥ †

It was late afternoon by the time they finished lunch and returned to the hotel, where Mrs. Sterling sat in the parlor room with her sketchbook open to a page depicting what looked like some kind of fossilized plant. She had her watercolors out, and the tips of her fingers bore multicolored stains. Her hair shone like copper wire under the gaslight, streaked with pale white, as she turned with a smile upon Jane and Terence's entrance. The only way she and Jane resembled one another was their eyes, green in color and always crinkled at the corners with some sort of emotion. Elation, despair, worry, exhaustion. There was always a crease of some kind there. They otherwise more resembled old colleagues rather than a mother and daughter.

"About time you two came back. Come and warm yourselves, children, you look chilled!" She said, brushing her hands as she stood to greet them. She must've noticed their rosy noses and cheeks, much in the same way that Jane caught something hinting at a catty knowing flickering across her grin.

Jane felt a sudden chill across her shoulders in the absence of Terence's heat when he took a step back toward the door. She bit her tongue to withhold an urge to whimper.

"Ah, thank you, Mrs. Sterling, but it's almost evening. I ought to leave you ladies to enjoy your night. The marshes of Wolf's Run can be a beast to navigate at night once you can no longer see the road," Terence said, lips pursed.

Both women shared a frown.

"Well, if you insist, Mr. Hayes," Mrs. Sterling said.

"We will see you again—soon—yes?" Jane's words emerged as a whine. She wasn't fond of the idea of him leaving quite yet, and, desperately seeking an excuse, added, "Y-you mentioned having fossils you'd want my father to see."

Their luncheon hadn't been anything spectacular, but Jane wasn't ready to have their time together come to an end. Lunch was at a simple cafe on a street neighboring the gardens, lined with brown storefronts Terence walked her through, though she couldn't recall the name of the road nor any of the stores, only that everything was gray and colorless. And cold. She'd been grateful that Terence's body was so warm, and that he didn't seem to mind her pressed against him. In the end, his eagerness to show her shops that had gowns and hats and shoes displayed in their windows was enough to make her smile. He was making an effort, and that was what mattered most to her.

The excursion and their lunch of tea and sandwiches was rather boring, with simple conversations consisting of Terence asking what her trip across the Atlantic was like, what she thought of Cambridge so far, what she'd thought of the gardens, and if she saw anything that piqued her interest in any of the store windows.

"Do all English women allow themselves to dress so..." she waved her hand in an attempt to capture a word that floated in the air around her, then used her pointed gaze to gesture to two young girls that strode past where they sat at the window. Both of them wore brown, so muted and dry that they nearly blended into the slick street. Their hats were small, and they wore jackets that hung well past their knees. *Practical*. That was the word Jane needed, but it wasn't what she wanted. "Drab?" was what she finally settled for as she wrinkled her nose, settled her chin on the heel of her palm, and watched the girls cross the street.

From the lip of his cup, Terence glanced between her and the girls. For a moment his gaze lingered on her chest, on her trilobite charm, to which Jane arched her back to puff her chest out further; the necklace itself was a similar shade of brown, but she knew she could make such a color flourish.

"I'm afraid I wouldn't know," he said. He then gestured to his own dark wardrobe and tilted his head. "Do you think of me as drab?"

"But of course!" She said and pinched the edge of his sleeve between a thumb and forefinger. "Have you ever considered that you'd look charming in green? Maybe even a fuschia color."

"Do you think so?" He looked at himself with a pinched brow, as if imagining himself in said colors.

Certainly. "Maybe," she shrugged and pinched his coat again.

She couldn't deny the comfort his company brought, especially after being denied an opportunity to further converse with him beyond simple introductions at May's exhibition. The idea of never seeing him again before the Sterlings were to leave England made something in her heart grow heavy. She was just starting to dig her claws into a man free of the influence of her sisters and mother, to at last have a companion wholly to herself… she couldn't let him go yet!

Mrs. Sterling looked between them both, eyes wide with a curious hunger. "Oh? Fossils, you say?"

"He told me that he found fossils in his garden, you see," Jane explained for Terence before he even had a chance to speak for himself. "And he was hoping Father could appraise them for their value and decipher what fossils they are. With your permission, I would love to have a look at these fossils."

"Please don't fret over the matter on my behalf, Jane," Terence interjected, perhaps a little too quickly. "I was merely curious about what value they may hold."

"Oh! Dear, you won't need Simon for a job like that," Mrs. Sterling made a gesture toward her daughter. "Jane would be of great help to you if you need something identified. She's been watching Simon work all her life. Everything he could possibly know, she would know as well."

Jane flushed but couldn't stop from holding herself a little higher. She did know her fossils, that much Mrs. Sterling had correct, though her truth may have been exaggerated. Jane was unsure if she would be able to provide Terence with an accurate analysis of the bones, not without her father's knowing eyes. But if this meant spending more time with him...

"No, no, I wouldn't wish to trouble Jane that way," he said, and though Jane's heart ached at the words, she was emboldened by the fact that he didn't scoff or laugh at the notion of a woman knowing her fossils.

Mrs. Sterling snorted. "Oh, please, we insist! What else is a girl to do around Cambridge?"

Croquet, walks in the park, visiting the museum—again, Jane thought, but what enjoyment would she get out of them if she didn't have a companion (who wasn't her mother) to share them with?

"Just for a day, then? How about tomorrow? Unless you're pre-occupied..." Mrs. Sterling said with a prim arch of her auburn brows.

Terence licked his lips as he looked between the two women. A damp sweat beaded at his temples, making his dark hair and graying sideburns glisten. Lines around his mouth deepened.

Why is he so bothered by the idea of a simple house visit? Surely living in a marsh doesn't seem so bad... And besides, I'm not that horrible of a guest! Jane inwardly huffed to distract herself from the rising worry that Terence would turn down her mother's offer, and thus they would never see each other again.

"Please, Terence?" She stepped forward and fluttered lashes in a toying blink, just as she had done when convincing him to sit beside her at yesterday's lecture.

The same shadow of a leashed dog returned to his gaze, softening it as he looked at her. That peculiar sadness started to leak through her again, just as it did at the greenhouse. She hoped such sadness was because he, too, was aware of how this could be the last chance they'd see each other if he turned down her offer.

Eventually, to her relief, he nodded. "Alright. I shall be back in the morning. Early. Five or six o'clock? I wish for you to have all day to work, Jane."

Mrs. Sterling smiled. "Oh, that'd be perfect!" She held Jane's shoulders. "We shall see you tomorrow, then, Mr. Hayes."

"Yes, I shall look forward to it," he ducked his head in a nod and secured his hat back on. As he turned to leave, he paused and looked at Jane. His mouth faltered once more into that wry grin, soft and plush at its edges. "Thank you for the company today, Jane. I hope to share many more with you before you're gone."

She had no chance to wave or offer her own thanks—which sat eagerly on the tip of her tongue—before he left them with a wordless stride.

She didn't know how to feel other than a newfound hollowed longing, so she just turned to face her mother. She narrowed her eyes when Mrs. Sterling's grin turned mischievous.

"Were you *actually* sleeping this morning, Mother?" she asked, and Mrs. Sterling only smirked before returning to her paints.

Three

THE MARSHES OF WOLF'S RUN SPANNED FAR INTO THE horizons on either side of the narrow dirt road.

It was an ocean of limply wavering grass and congealed puddles of slop, and all Jane could see through a creeping fog so thick that it blotted out the sun were crosses. There were hundreds of them, sprouted from the mud in sprigs of rust, wood, and stone that the carriage carelessly rattled past every couple of yards.

Jane's mouth ran dry and her palms sweated within her gloves as she wondered how many of them marked the placement of a body.

Peat ensured that a corpse drowned in a bog would be preserved, making it into something of a mummy. And the more Jane thought of a potential hoard of mummified dead haunting the depths of the marsh, the more she fiddled with the trilobite necklace between her fingers. Once she imagined Terence's brother's grave being somewhere out in those reedy waters, she decided she was dwelling on the subject too much.

"The villagers believe they bring protection," Terence's voice startled her free of her morbid daydreaming as they passed a crudely made wooden cross with several rosaries draped across it. He had been abnormally silent during the ride north from Cambridge, and it waned Jane's initial excitement about this whole trip into indistinguishable nerves. He was ill at ease, but not because of her. It was something else, she knew it, but not knowing what that something else was made her ill at ease, too.

The leers of the locals did little to alleviate those pins and needles prickling beneath her skin.

As they passed through Wolf's Run—a gray little village bisected down its center by a road that branched into a spiderweb of alleyways, walls of mills, brick huts, a pub, a post office, a church with a bent steeple, and a graveyard—those who had been on the street abandoned chores of stringing laundry and sweeping front stoops to rush inside, where they then peeked from between their curtains to burn their stares into Jane. Those who remained on the road went still as they watched the cab roll past, lips curled, eyes dark. Jane wished Terence sat beside her so she could turn and hide against his shoulder.

As much as she tried to shake away the sensation, the sight of the multitude of crosses paired with Terence's silence made it cling to her with cold, sticky fingers.

Protection against what? she questioned behind sealed lips as they passed another cross, rusted and bent.

"Are any of them bodies?" she asked instead. Not that she feared the undead. Though she never carried weapons with her, she at least had a hairpin that, when unsheathed, bore a wicked little blade. A weapon such as that would suffice when fending off the undead, wouldn't it? Her confidence wavered into oblivion as she reached into her bag to grasp the pin, nestled among the textbook and parchment she'd packed that morning, and the silver bent slightly in her grip.

Terence held her gaze for a moment, something abstruse burbling in his eyes' dark depths, before murmuring a gentle, "I do not know. I'd rather not think of it."

The carriage rocked as it continued down the road, kicking up thick mud beneath its wheels. The road was long and thin, being only wide enough to fit a single carriage, as it wound its way through the marshes to what the locals had christened, according to Terence, "the Drowning House."

Jane had wondered why they would've called it that, but then she saw the approaching hill that arose from the water before them. Atop it was a house jutting upward from the earth with the lop-sidedness of a cracked incisor. The closer they got, the more sparse the crosses became, as if whoever had been planting them was too afraid to dare take a step closer to the house. Jane gripped the knife even tighter as they passed the final cross, a rather primitive one made of sticks and twine. What had made the house so horrible in the first place that not even some vandal armed with crucifixes felt safe enough to approach?

And why are we approaching?

Rain pattered against the carriage as it rolled to a stop before a set of stone steps, and Jane stared up at the house with a seedling of disappointment planted in her belly. It looked painfully ordinary, with what appeared to be rot gnawing away at the brick siding, darkening the exterior with some blank, moldering infection.

The house was two stories high and geometric in shape, with four windows on the first floor, four on the second, and a modest turret extended upward from its eastern wing. On its backside were arched, protruding windows that hinted at a conservatory, or even a greenhouse. Also behind the house was a wilted garden and a small bundle of trees that Jane supposed was a forest. Too many ravens roosted in the bare branches in cawing bundles of night-colored feathers.

"Welcome to the Drowning House," Terence said, offering her an apologetic smile. He must've caught the instinctual curl of her lip because he sighed. "I wish I were able to present you with something more grand. But I can assure you that it isn't so terrible once you're inside."

He stepped from the carriage, hunched his shoulders to shield himself from the rain, and held out a hand to Jane.

Very softly, he whispered, "Watch your step," as she hopped down to join him on the wet, hungry earth. She resisted a wince as mud stained the pastel pink of her skirts. The dampness from the mud was already seeping through her boots, her stockings, deep into her flesh.

"The place is huge," she remarked, allowing Terence to usher her toward it. They left Ruben to bring the mare (who he had introduced as "Mistletoe" when Jane asked) and carriage to the stables on a corner of the property. "Has it always been in your family?"

Terence opened the door and stepped aside so she may enter first once she finished cleaning the mud from her boots with the iron scraper just outside the threshold.

"I do not know, unfortunately. It has just always... *been* here, from a time before even my father was a boy, I think," he said. "A phantom that rose from the marshes' depths, is what the locals say. That is why they call it the Drowning House: it is a house that is, or at least once was, perpetually drowning in the swamp."

Jane only nodded to his words as she looked around the entrance hall. The place was immaculate in its cleanliness, with floors so newly washed that the smell of vinegar and lemon juice lingered in the air, and was illuminated by frosted glass sconces. She hated the wallpaper, which was a sad shade of periwinkle-blue. She never really liked blue as a color, it reminded her too much of the isolation of oceans and lakes—it was a color that inspired only feelings of loneliness. That was how she would describe the Drowning House thus far: lonely, and perhaps even artificial in how clean it was.

She grimaced whilst running a finger along the paper's flowering, leafy pattern, and instead found herself tracing what felt like a deep groove beneath the paper. Too deep, too long, too parallel with the trimming to be a simple rotting of the wood, especially when she splayed her fingers against the wall and each of her four fingers found themselves almost perfectly nestled in more of the marks. Jane couldn't help but speculate that they had been clawed in by an animal.

An opossum or a raccoon in the walls, perhaps? Did England even have such critters?

She retracted, then, and eyed the faint indentations in the wallpaper, camouflaged by its pattern.

"I would've half-expected this place to be positively riddled with damp and mold," she said. *That is to say, it already isn't so underneath all that pretty paper.*

Terence laughed a bit, more to ease tension rather than out of genuine merriment, when he offered to take her coat. "Oh, believe me, Jane, this house isn't impervious to damp. I am just particular about cleanliness."

The jangling of metal and many keys announced her arrival long before a woman with a hawkish demeanor and pale gray hair tucked beneath a bonnet joined them in the hall. The smile she offered Jane was tight and showed little of her teeth, but her brown eyes held a kind warmth that unraveled the tension knotted between Jane's shoulders. A chatelaine jangled chunkily at her hip with every step she took, and when she stopped she clasped her hands before her. An overabundance of lace frills frothed from the woman's sleeves, hiding all but her fingertips.

"And such wouldn't be so if it weren't for the marvelous work of our own Mrs. Foster," Terence said warmly as he at last shucked off his coat.

"You flatter me, Mr. Hayes," the woman said, eyes shining as she then turned to Jane. She briefly squinted when she must've noticed Jane's shortly-cropped hair, but her friendliness did not falter. "We were informed that you were to be visiting for the day so we have everything all prepared for you in the sitting room. Ms. Hudson should have tea ready if you're at all in need of a refreshment, Miss Sterling."

"Thank you, that is very kind of you," Jane said.

Jane didn't know what to expect with the staff of this house, whether they'd be cold like the villagers or some bent-back hags birthed by the marshes with fungus sprouting from between their teeth, but it certainly wasn't this. It was welcoming and embraced her like a hug as Mrs. Foster led her down the hall behind the main stair and into a sitting room pleasantly heated by kindling in the fireplace. In one corner was a harpsichord, sitting opposite a set of armchairs, walls lined with neat bookshelves, and tall, latticed windows that opened to the yawning expanse of the marshes.

By the windows, Mrs. Foster and Terence presented Jane with a small desk, and atop that desk was an assortment of rocks set in as straight of a line as the organizer could muster.

However, Jane was instead drawn to the fireplace, and the little artifact situated atop it. Right in its center was a small statue, cast in gold to be in the shape of an erect humanoid with a veil draped over a misshapen, oblong head. She thought it to be an ugly little thing to have as a sole piece of decor.

Wishing to get a better look, she reached to grab it, but a hand on her shoulder pulled her away just as her fingertips grazed the statue. A spark coursed through her fingers, up her arm, and into her chest when she turned to see Terence behind her.

"The fossils, Jane," he said and nodded to the desk.

"The fossils?" Jane asked but then remembered one of the reasons why she begged to be here. She realized that probably made her appear even less of a professional, and she coughed out a haughty, "Oh, yes, of course—the fossils!" to stifle the blush that rose into her ears.

She crossed the room while shaking the tingling from her fingers and thoughts of the idol from her mind.

Terence hummed as he approached the desk beside her, lightly unfolding a crumpled corner of the cloth the rocks laid on.

"These were the fossils Ruben found in the garden the other day. I was sure that they're fossils because you see?" He traced his finger along frond-shaped imprints possessed by over half of the rocks, haunted by the ghosts of prehistoric ferns. "I just felt a great curiosity in knowing *what* these fossils may be, and what worth they may have."

Jane removed her spectacles from her purse and placed them on the tip of her nose (more to give her a scholarly air than practicality) before she took one of the fossils and held it up so she could better observe it in the light. The rock was dusty and gray amidst the bright pink fingers of her glove, and within it were the pale brown imprints of several fish-like skeletons. They were fish, yes, but what kind of fish? Was it even a fossil, or just a hundred-year-old bone? Was it one or many species of fish, eternally trapped together on the surface of a piece of loam? Jane ran her thumb over it just as her tongue did over her lips as she set the rock back on the desk.

When she turned, Terence and Mrs. Foster were looking at her almost expectantly. She took off her glasses to tap them against the heel of her palm. "I'll see what I can do! I must warn you that I don't possess nearly as much knowledge as my father does, and I hope my mother's enthusiasm hasn't raised your expectations or spirits too high."

"And I hope that you do not feel this task is too perilous or dire," Terence said.

Jane wanted to laugh. He spoke as though she were to undergo some grave quest rather than inspecting meager rocks.

"As I've previously explained, I am merely interested in these stones' identities for my own chance to learn, and I was too afraid of risking damage to them during transport. If your identifications happen to be incorrect, then it may be a chance for both of us to learn," he said as he ghosted his hand over the aligned rocks. He breathed a raspy chuckle as he then rubbed his brow. "I apologize, this all seems silly. I never anticipated having you come all this way out here to look at bloody *rocks*."

"It is no trouble, truly," Jane said and patted his shoulder, almost mirroring the friendly action she observed him share with Ruben. "I would much rather be occupied like this than be trapped in a hotel room with my mother in a city neither of us knows what to do in. Besides, all she would be doing is her watercolors. Have you ever been forced to endure the horrors of hours upon hours of watercolors? And in total silence, mind you! No music, not even humming or chit-chat."

"Sounds horrible," he sighed and scrubbed his hands against the thighs of his trousers. "I appreciate your enthusiasm, Jane. Now, I'm unsure of how much time you will require for your work, but this house is as much yours as it is mine in the meantime. We're like family here, and I ensure that guests are no exception."

Jane tried to maintain her smile as she tapped her glasses harder against her hand. As much as she appreciated the gesture, she worried he was overcompensating for something, but what that was she didn't know, and that made her uneasy the same way his silence in the carriage did. What had happened to the confident, soft-spoken Terence she had spoken to just yesterday?

As the idol watched over the three of them, sweat prickled at her collar.

"There's no need to worry yourself so. I'm grateful for the opportunity you've given me, Mr. Hayes," she took the moment to put on her glasses and push them up her nose using her knuckle, as a point of emphasis. "Let us get started, then, shall we?"

† †† ↓† † ↑† †↑† † ↑† ↓↑† ↓†† †

JANE'S BACK ACHED FROM BEING HUNCHED OVER THE DESK for what felt like too long of hours and her eyes burned from looking between the rocks and her father's books she'd brought with her. She had tried to have the habit of bringing one of the textbooks her father authored with her whenever she traveled, whether it be if she happened across an enthusiastic supporter of her father's in search of a signed copy or if she were bored and sought entertainment.

The Sterling Field Guide to Bygone Botany by Zelda Lizbeth Lemke-Sterling & Dr. Simon Howard Sterling, Ph.D., D. Sc., D.G.S. was a comprehensive manual, of sorts, as Dr. Sterling liked to describe it. It was a simple listing of known prehistoric flora (as of 1903), where they were discovered and by whom, and potential descendants in the modern world. Alongside descriptions were various illustrations, of both fossilized plants and hypothetical imaginings of what these things may have looked like in life, all done in Mrs. Sterling's ink etchings. Along the bottom margins of some pages were her footnotes justifying the creative reasonings behind her illustrations.

It was a passion project between man and wife, and in a way, it made Jane envious that such a thing could be born of passion and union, and still be celebrated despite a woman's name being the first one seen on the cover. Jane always held a residual envy regarding the endeavors of her mother and sisters; men wanted women with artistic talent, not intelligence. They wanted a thing to entertain them, make their hours pass by, not to challenge or outwit them. That was why Jane had come to cherish Terence's company: he listened. He remained quiet, never curling his lip in distaste, when she spoke. Such silence was encouraging in its rarity, and his kindness even more so. Even if he were a little awkward.

Terence attempted to give her space as she worked but she could feel the schoolboy's curiosity radiating from him whenever he lingered in the sitting room's doorway or entered the room to ask if she needed another cup of tea every five minutes. During several of those trips, he stepped just close enough to peek her over her shoulder, close enough that his breath disturbed the hair over her ear before Jane would smirk and hunch over to shield her notes from him.

"Ah! Naughty boy! No peeking!"

At the sound of her cackle, he'd rush from the room with heavy steps. She would soon lapse back into silence when her laughter echoed back to her in empty mockery. The house didn't seem to take kindly to merriment.

She at least appreciated Terence's little game of curiosity. His audience was certainly preferred over that of utter silence and the idol that leered at her from atop the mantle. As much as she wished to study it, she found that she couldn't look upon the idol for too long before her neck turned clammy and an ache blossomed in the fingertips that brushed against it. She lacked the courage to ask Terence where he acquired such an ugly heirloom.

The third time Terence entered the room, he didn't approach her from behind. Instead, Jane heard him fumbling with something, which was followed by a strange sound that she could only describe as a plastic, rubbery vacuuming of air. When she finally looked over her shoulder to investigate, the crackling twang of a harpsichord and violin duet filled the air, belched forth from the maw of a phonograph Terence stood beside in the room's shadowed corner. He held a cylindrical holding container in his hands as he looked between the phonograph and Jane.

"I thought you'd appreciate Bach over silence," he said. "He is a personal favorite of mine. A better symphony than rain on windows, I'd imagine."

Jane was enamored with the phonograph as she watched the wax cylinder spin, and her brain tried to puzzle how a needle tracing its etchings could produce such music. She desperately wished to know how it worked, just as she wished to know how bones fit and operated within a dinosaur.

Until now, Jane had never been in the presence of a phonograph. Or, well, at least one that was operational. She'd see them in the homes of her father's acquaintances in the more respectable suburbs of Milwaukee, like Downer Woods, where polished streets shone with golden lamps and cobbled stones that glimmered in their cleanliness.

Terence suddenly looked down, brow pinched and mouth tight, when he must've misinterpreted her awed silence for displeasure. "I-If you'd wish to change it I've the music of Liszt, Vivaldi, Dvořák, Bizet, Grieg, Beethoven—"

"Terence, I assure you, Bach is fine enough," Jane said, rising from her chair so that she may approach the phonograph. Her body popped and cracked as she stretched, grateful for the chance to at last move. She didn't dare *touch* the device, but she did ghost her fingers over its tonearm, the horn that vibrated with music. "I've just never seen one of these things work before. Y'know, my father once owned one. Never had a chance to work it, though."

"Oh? How come?"

"Back home, each of us sisters has a pet: Meredith has Patroclus the hound, Emmy has her daughters Titania and Ophelia, and I suppose her husband Ethan is enough of a pet, and I have Mr. Thompson. He's this orange tom I found in our rubbish a couple years back, and he has a proclivity to hunt and chase, but only after dust bunnies. Would be a cold day in Hell before he'd be a proper cat and hunt a bird.

"So, anyway, you see, he had been chasing one of those dust bunnies through Father's study when his tail knocked into the leg of the stand holding the phonograph and then—" Jane mimicked an explosion with her hands, "*Crash*! Thing broke into a thousand shards! It broke in ways I never thought it possible for wood and metal to break! It truly was an epic mess; words alone fail to do it justice."

As she told her story, Terence had taken a seat in one of the armchairs, leaning forward, chin held in a hand supported on his knee. "Oh, how dreadful... I can't imagine the rage he must've felt."

"Oh, of course, he was *furious*. Twenty dollars lay shattered on his study floor, and not once did he have a chance to play any of his cylinders—which he paid about ten bucks a piece for, y'know!" Jane seated herself on the arm of the loveseat adjacent to Terence, her back to the dwindling fireplace—and the idol's burning stare. "That evening he burst into my room, Mr. Thompson hiding on my lap, and he declared—" she put her hands on her hips and puffed out her chest, broadening her shoulders, in a crude caricature of her father. She puckered her lips, trying to feign the image of his black-and-silver bottlebrush mustache, and bellowed in a nasal baritone, "'*Janie!* Your wretched little flea-bitten nuisance has cost me a fortune! He owes me a new phonograph, that heathen! Send him to find work as a mouser, for he shall forever be in debt with me!'"

Terence chuckled, muffling his smirk behind a broad hand. "What of Mr. Thompson's debt? Does he still owe your father?"

"Very much so. And he's been accruing overdue fees."

"Ah, how unfortunate," he said softly.

The din of Bach's duet spiraled to an end, leaving only the sound of wind and rain rattling the windows to occupy its air, as Jane and Terence held each other's stare.

Whenever he smiled, lopsided and gentle, Jane noticed a dimple form in the center of his chin, and it took every fiber of willpower to not reach forward and tap said dimple—and with a fingertip or her lips, she would never say.

"Can we give Vivaldi a try?" She said, clearing her throat and glancing at the phonograph to break free of such traitorous temptations. She stepped up to it and snatched the first canister she saw. "I wish to see *how* those cylinders work."

┆┼┼╷│┆┼╵│┼╷│┆┼┆╷┆

As afternoon dimmed beneath the oncoming twilight, a storm had started to claw at the house. Thunder growled through the skies, between the clouds, rattling the Drowning House to its very foundations. Rain slashed across the windows with a sharpness Jane felt cut down to her bones.

And as the daylight faded, so did Terence's friendliness. With every hour that had come to pass, the more he chose to silently brood at the sitting room windows, watching the skies, the rain, the marshes, with a deep crease to his brow. He had stopped tending to the phonograph hours ago, leaving Jane to steep in the house's increasingly tense silence.

Jane was freed from her spell of working with the fossils (which had come to primarily consist of mindlessly transcribing notes related to what she had come to identify in an attempt to appear busy) when he cleared his throat and stepped away from the window.

"I think it might be best that we return you to Cambridge," he said, offering her a tightening of his lips that might have been a smile. Whatever it was, it failed to summon the dimple to his chin.

Jane stretched back in her chair with her arms arched over her head. She removed her glasses by pushing them up so that they could rest in her hair. "I didn't realize it was already so late."

"One of many cruel games played by darkness," Terence uttered with a tone so low and so cold it gave her pause. "Pray that a road is still out there."

"I... can certainly try," Jane said, never having been a woman of religion or prayer. She cleared her throat, "So, the fossils I think you may have here are—"

"Why don't we discuss this tomorrow, Jane?"

She flinched at his interruption and tamed a scowl by biting her lower lip. She tapped her pen against the rocks before her (two of which she marked as being ammonites, one being a still unidentified fish, one as the imprint of *Psaronius* fronds, and another was the potential scaly imprint of a *Lepidodendron* tree; none of which were high-value finds, but Jane had been excited to identify them nonetheless). "But, you see, I can bring these—"

"*Tomorrow*, Jane," his hands braced the desk. They shivered so intensely that the rocks rattled. Even the veins just below his skin seemed to writhe. Sweat pearled along his temple as his gaze on her remained unmoving. "Please."

Is a storm truly that frightening? Jane would've found Terence's apparent fear of thunder and rain adorable if he weren't staring at her with the grimness of a fresh funeral.

"Alright, then..." she said as she tried to swallow down a prickle of disappointment, a stab of betrayal.

She packed her things in silence, leaving only the rocks and her father's book on the desk, excuses for her to return to the house tomorrow. Mrs. Foster, who seemingly disappeared as the skies outside grew darker, had Jane's coat and hat waiting for her in the foyer.

"Will I see you tomorrow then?" Jane asked, eagerly looking up at Terence as they waited for Ruben to retrieve the cab.

The worry that'd previously chilled his features softened, and his mouth twitched in a weary grin. It wasn't until her hand started to overheat that she realized that he gently gripped her fingers. "I couldn't wish for such to come sooner, Jane."

Ruben came to the door, his coat already soaking wet, and gestured for Jane to join him underneath his newfound umbrella. Mud sucked at Jane's boots as they crossed the lawn, threatening to vacuum her into the depths of the earth with every step.

"See you tomorrow, Terence!" She shouted over the rain before hauling herself into the cab. A hopeful promise, even if he didn't call back to her.

A soothing cacophony of rain drummed against all sides of the carriage as Jane rested her head back against the seat with a sigh.

As much as the sudden curtness in Terence's attitude and his urgency for her to leave perplexed (and, admittedly, to a lesser degree, hurt) her, she couldn't deny the satisfaction she felt about the work she had done today—and the time she'd spent with him.

Whenever she pictured the warmth of his eyes, the timid

twitch of his lips as he allowed himself a smile, the heat of his shadow over her shoulder, a hot, tingling pit wriggled in her stomach. She craved more. More of him, his attention—his praise. Anticipation for tomorrow's visit made her shiver in her seat.

Hopefully whatever foul mood ails him now will be long gone in the morning!

The ardor that thrummed in her soul was snuffed out when she was suddenly launched forward and crashed into the opposite bench. The carriage lurched once more, throwing her to the floor as she tried to right herself, before coming to an abrupt stop. The horse screamed outside. Pain blossomed in Jane's cheek where her teeth bit down deep into flesh. She choked at the sudden taste of blood bathing her tongue.

As she stood, she struggled to find proper footing with the carriage's newfound lopsidedness, leaning too far forward and canted to the left at a severe angle. She pushed open the door and yelped when a slurry of mud poured into the interior, ice cold and thick. The carriage was half-drowned in muck. Mistletoe, too, was trapped as her vicious bucking sucked her deeper into the mud. Ruben was pulling on her reins in an attempt to free her.

Jane abandoned her bag in the carriage and rushed to Ruben's side. Her hands closed over his as she joined him in pulling. Effort stressed her arms and between her shoulders, and she struggled to maintain a grip with her rain-slick gloves.

When Mistletoe showed no signs of even coming loose, Ruben dropped to his knees, plunged his hands into the earth, and started to dig her out. Jane gritted her teeth and continued to yank on the reins.

The mud gave a viscous slurp as Mistletoe launched herself free, taking Jane off her feet and nearly trampling her in her escape. The mare continued to kick and shake as she stamped back toward the Drowning House.

"You all right, Miss Sterling?" Ruben gripped Jane's arm and hoisted her back onto her feet.

Jane shivered and sputtered mud from her lips but she managed a meek nod. She'd properly mourn her stained clothes once she was warm and dry.

Ruben sighed and ran a hand through his own dirtied hair.

"The marshes are flooded," he remarked, chewing on his lip as he glanced back at the sinking carriage; with another shiver, Jane hurried to retrieve her bag from the wreckage, holding it close to her chest.

Water crept toward the outermost fringes of the lawn. Lightning clawed across the sky in a blinding strike, and what Jane saw was no longer a marsh but rather a raging sea. She saw no road, no land. There were only distant reeds and those damned crosses bowed beneath another harsh gust of wind.

Once more, Ruben's hand found its way through his hair. "Mr. Hayes won't like this," he groaned.

"Well, *I* certainly wouldn't like seeing my front lawn flooded like this," Jane said, a shiver running through her as rain further soaked through her dress.

Ruben didn't laugh, or even smirk. He stared into the tempest of frothing mud and water with the silence of a man sentenced to death.

CHAPTER

Four

THE DISPIRITED WARMTH OF THE DROWNING HOUSE failed to soothe Jane's shivering as she stepped into the foyer.

Rain and mud dripped off her in fat tears to paint the floor with earthy stains. She winced at her mess and decided that she would offer to clean it for Mrs. Foster. After removing her hat (and taking a moment to mourn how sadly the tinseled feathers drooped), she shook any remaining dampness from her hair.

From deeper within the house was the resounding opening and closing of a door, followed by a chorus of exasperated gasps and frightened murmuring. Jane hurried down the hall to join them.

When she entered the kitchen, Mrs. Foster, the cook Ms. Hudson, and Terence were huddled around Ruben, faces pale and worry etched into their brows. The two women looked as though they were prepared to leave, draped in cloaks and gripping umbrellas. If the seething hisses sharpening their whispers meant anything, they weren't enthused that they couldn't leave sooner— or rather at all.

Jane tapped a knuckle against the wooden chopping block in the kitchen's center, and all whipped their attention to her so fiercely she swore she heard bones snap. Whatever color remained in their faces leached away in an instant. Silence echoed against the kitchen's tiles, broken only by a rumbling chuckle of thunder outside.

She showed them her palms and flashed her teeth in a smile. "Easy, now, I'm no ghost," she then made a rueful gesture to the mud trailing behind her. "If you'll allow me a couple minutes I'll clean this for you—"

Terence had crossed the room and took hold of her arm, not hard enough to bruise, but she knew she couldn't break away even if she wanted to. "You must leave," he said in a voice that creaked behind his teeth.

Jane popped her lips open to speak, but Ruben interjected with an exacerbated groan.

"And where to, Mr. Hayes? I already told you: the road was flooded," he raised a hand toward a window blotted by the storm's darkness before slapping it down against trousers thick with mud. "We were barely able to get Mistletoe freed and it'd be a miracle if the cab isn't wholly drowned by now."

"We nearly drowned ourselves," Jane added pointedly. Clumps of mud started to crust in her hair, beneath her nails. "Do you expect me to trek all the way back to Wolf's Run while your swamp of a yard is trying to eat me whole?"

"We will all need to stay the night," Ruben muttered; Mrs. Foster and Ms. Hudson lost their pallor before exchanging more choked whimpers. "Roads are washed out, and we've no transport."

Terence at last let go of Jane and raked a hand through his

hair, inhaling deeply. His lips were white as if he were on the verge of throwing up. He looked to his staff with another shuddering sigh. "You three know what to do, and I expect you to show Jane to a guest room, please," he dismissed them with a curt nod. "Rest safely, all of you."

Jane's throat suddenly went dry and she squeezed her hands atop her chest. *Know how to do what?*

He waited for them all to clear out, and it was Mrs. Foster, still in a dark riding cloak, who replaced his grip on Jane's arm, ushering her from the kitchen as he watched them go.

"What was that all about?" Jane whispered.

When Mrs. Foster failed to offer an immediate answer, instead choosing to fidget with the lace of her sleeves, Jane frowned. The woman gnawed on her thin lip for a moment before finally speaking, "Mr. Hayes is just anxious about the storm. He cares for us deeply, as you can see, and would rather us not travel in the night and the rain. We're the only family we have for one another, and he wants to do what's best for our safety, Miss Sterling. I know little of what superstitions you Americans hold but here in Wolf's Run we fear the night—and all the things birthed in its darkness."

"Rightfully so." Ms. Hudson sniffed as they made their way upstairs. Her auburn brow was settled in a glowering line.

"Georgianna!" Mrs. Foster seethed in warning.

"We got ourselves three rules around here for at night," Ms. Hudson continued, looking at Jane. "If you think you have heard something outside your window, draw the curtains and return to bed; do not look too deep into the darkness, for it *will* stare right back at you; and, most importantly, never, *ever* leave your room until you are certain that is daylight that spills across your bedspread." She held up a thick finger as she listed each rule. "I do not know what darkness you Americans know of, but here you must be afraid of the dark, respect whatever lives in the dark because the dark wants to hunt you, it wants to gut you—"

"*Georgianna*, that is enough!" Mrs. Foster hissed again, gripping Jane's shoulders to steer her down the hall toward a washroom; the hallway was as soulless and sad as the rest of the house with its periwinkle wallpaper and absence of decor.

The cook only grumbled in response before trudging to one of the several doors lining the hallway.

What would happen if I felt like leaving my room at night? Jane wanted to ask out of defiance and to dampen the worried flame smoldering in her throat. *Certainly, the world wouldn't end, would it?*

In the washroom was a claw-footed tub along a wall with large, arching windows facing the darkness of the marshes. Lightning illuminated pale tiles that smelled of the same over-powering vinegar cleaning solution as in the entrance hall. What looked to be rusted stains oozed down the linoleum in tails of dark brown, as if the walls had once bled.

"Wash up, quickly, and we will find night clothes for you, Miss Sterling," Mrs. Foster said and started running water.

"But what of Ruben?" Jane asked, already undressing down to her chemise. Urgency—along with anxiety inspired by Ms. Hudson's warnings and everyone's seemingly newfound panic—fueled her limbs, making every movement a fevered jerk. "Shouldn't he have a chance to clean and warm himself in the bath as well?"

The smell of jasmine and clove permeated the air as Mrs. Foster added soap to the bath—too much of it, Jane decided, as the scents had come to be overpowering.

"There is no time—" (*No time?* Jane swallowed in a silent plea for answers.) "He will be alright, Miss Sterling, now wash up— *quickly!*" Mrs. Foster was swift in her departure once she, word-lessly, gathered Jane's soiled clothing and left her to bathe.

Wind rattled the windows as Jane sank into the water, savoring the heat that burned her skin. She thought about her mother, then, as she began to scrub away mud with her nails, and worried. No one would have been able to inform Mrs. Sterling as to why Jane hadn't returned to the hotel. She hadn't caught sight of or heard any signs of a telegraph or phone wired in the house. Surely Mrs. Sterling wouldn't mind her being gone for one night, and with respectable company, too. The Sterlings weren't as inclined to seeing men and women together—alone—and assuming some sort of scandal.

Scandal.

Jane's fingers paused clawing away filth. She wondered if whatever caused the sudden panic that'd gripped the house was something scandalous. As much as she enjoyed the gossip of a good scandal, she refrained from ruminating on the idea for too long as she wasn't quite ready to sour her image of Terence just yet and she wished to enjoy this bath, no matter how fleeting or strange its circumstances were.

By morning, the storm would be over and Jane would be brought back to Cambridge in one piece. She tried to ignore the creeping sadness chilling the bathwater as she started to realize that this would be the first time she was to spend a night somewhere without any family. No mother or father, no Meredith or Emmy, not even Mr. Thompson. For the first time in her twenty-four years, she was utterly alone. And, to her surprise, she hated it. As much as her sisters were competition and her mother an incessant whisper, they were comforting constants, they were her companions and family nonetheless.

It felt like only seconds passed before Mrs. Foster returned with a white nightgown draped in the crook of her arm.

"Out, Miss Sterling, out," she shooed Jane along. Some strands of hair had come undone from her bonnet, giving her an even more frazzled appearance, as she assisted Jane out of the tub and into the awaiting nightgown.

"I'm not taking this from anyone, am I?" Jane asked as the dress hung loosely from her frame, so long that it trailed on the floor behind her. She held a heavy fistful of fabric to ensure she wouldn't trip on the excess skirt. A mane of dusty lace made her throat and jawline itch.

"Oh, no, no. This house has seen a plethora of staff, and some things are bound to be left behind," Mrs. Foster said a little too simply.

She led Jane to a circular, desolate room. The wallpaper was the same lonely periwinkle-blue as the rest of the house, as were the sheets on the narrow bed. Jane's bag sat beside the nightstand, upon which was a single gas lamp. There was no other furniture or decoration. The air smelled of dust and melancholy. It was a sight more fitting to a sanitorium cell than an Englishman's estate. Not at all like her room back in Milwaukee, with its coral-colored wallpaper, plush pink bedspreads, and a view of Lake Michigan she could observe from a balcony she had decorated with roses and lilies in the summer months.

Jane resisted the urge to grimace. Her first night alone, and *this* was where she was expected to sleep?

"Right," Mrs. Foster said, and she fumbled with the keys on her chatelaine. "I pray that you rest safely, Miss Sterling."

Before Jane could even turn to thank Mrs. Foster for her kindness or to bid her a good-night, the door slammed shut, plunging the room into darkness, and the key turned in the lock with a resounding clank.

CHAPTER

Five

A SOUND LIKE THUNDER RATTLED THROUGH THE ROOM and startled Jane out of an otherwise dreamless sleep.

Panic spiked through her heart when she failed to recognize her surroundings, but as she focused on the deep blue of the wallpaper, the creaking sighs of the Drowning House's bones, and the thrum of rain against its windows, she crumpled back into the stale smell of even staler sheets with a groan.

Right. The Drowning House, the storm, the flooded marshes. It all washed back over her in an ebbing wave of cold mud.

She groaned and scrubbed the heel of her palm into her eye sockets. It had taken her what felt like half an age to at last fall asleep. The caterwauling storm paired with the dusty old bed and its squealing springs, the unease worming its way through her, and her stomach groaning from lack of dinner, Jane failed to find enough comfort to properly sleep. She tried to imagine Mr. Thompson's warmth or the sound of her mother's snores, but the absence of both made her feel all the colder beneath paper-thin sheets.

She sighed and lay flat on her back. Her eyes traced the cracks branching across the plaster ceiling to attempt to restart the cycle of sleeplessness.

Was Terence also struggling to sleep? Was he tossing and turning in his bed, eyes weary from the frustration of being unable to rest them? She grinned at the sudden thought of going on a journey in search of his bedroom to ask if she could crawl into bed with him where she would then latch onto him and his heat and comfort. He probably wouldn't hesitate in offering her bed to him. Not in a sexual manner, but rather because such was the law of a gentleman: you sacrifice a bit of yourself for the good of a lady. Jane liked to think he was the breed of gentleman who would skin himself alive and wrap his flesh around her shoulders if it meant keeping her warm for just a moment.

Grim as the image was, Jane hummed with a little grin as she burrowed deep into the mattress to pretend that instead of creaky springs she laid atop a sculpted chest and was held by strong arms rather than dusty blankets.

Her heartbeat and breathing had started to fall into a tired rhythm, and her eyelids began to weigh themselves closed, when that thundering sound once more shook the room down to its very floorboards. This time, it was accompanied by the scraping of something against wood, long and slow—against her door, as whatever lurked on the other side took its time in trying to claw its way inside. A dog begging for scraps. Who in the house had a dog? Jane couldn't recall seeing one...

The scratching continued, but only for a moment before it halted, and the silence that followed was deafening.

Jane nearly released the breath she was holding, too afraid to let it go, before a low moan droned from the other side of the door. It was a groan with a dreadful gurgle she felt bubble in the back of her own throat, a sound that seemingly couldn't decide between being a human wail or a beast's growl. Whatever it was, Jane didn't move, only clutching a fistful of sheets against her chin.

The storm continued to seethe just beyond her window, and a flash of lighting proved that she was alone in the room. But that didn't tell her who—*what*—was scratching against the door. She wasn't sure if she even wanted to know what was on the other side; bliss lay in not knowing.

Another moan pressed against the wood, another agonizingly long scrape of nails dragged across the door until Jane felt those unseen claws raking down the plains of her ribs, pleading with her to be let inside.

Who are you? Her lips couldn't muster the courage to call out to the intruder and she instead choked on the ice-cold fear lodged firmly at the back of her tongue.

"Mrs. Foster?" she somehow mustered. "Mrs. Foster, is that you? Ruben?"

Nothing. Only more scratching.

Slowly, Jane rose out of bed. Had an animal gotten into the house? Perhaps some vagabond in need of shelter from the storm? Curiosity was screaming in the back of her mind, demanding to know what was on the other side, and why they had the audacity to disturb her slumber.

She lit the oil lamp, bathing the room in a dim yellow light that turned the wallpaper a murky shade of green. The scratching continued as she neared the door. To temper her rising anxiety, she tried to picture some great, but harmless, dog on the other side, perhaps a lost Newfoundland or Great Dane, just looking for a midnight snack after it accidentally wandered from home and into another that wasn't its own. Hot, damp air rushed from the crack at the bottom of the door, as if a curious snout snuffled along it.

Ms. Hudson's warnings echoed within the depths of her skull, then.

Ignore things that speak from the darkness—don't leave your bedroom until you are certain it is sunlight spilling across your sheets.

The warnings tamed her temptation and she kept her eager hand closed into a tight fist against her chest. What if it wasn't a lost dog?

She stared at the door and the shadow that shuffled along its bottom. It was a shadow that swayed, only telling Jane that whatever was on the other side was real, or real enough to cast a shadow.

But there was one other thing that kept her from opening the door. The knob was already turning itself. Her heart lurched in her throat.

She anticipated the door to open as it jerked within its frame, but it didn't give way. Mrs. Foster's lock held firm, but Jane was unsure if a lock could keep whatever was on the other side at bay, especially as the door's shaking grew in its intensity. The moaning devolved into vicious snarls, the scratching into a clawing violence.

Jane rushed back to the sanctuary of the rickety bed that squealed in protest beneath her sudden weight. On the nightstand, she rifled through her bag until her hand closed over something cold and thin, and she pulled out the silver hairpin. She took the metal sheath, twisted it, and withdrew the hidden knife. It was a gift her grandmother had given to all the Sterling daughters after their first monthly bleedings, a tool to defend, a piece of beauty that could be honed into a weapon, and Jane wore it in her hair everywhere she went. But as she grew older, yet to face an opponent that'd require such a weapon, it had turned into a conversational piece, made even more so after she cut her hair on her twentieth birthday.

But now, as she hid beneath the covers with the knife clutched tight against her chest, she failed to find security in its presence as she listened to the intruder pounding at the bedroom door. If she held doubts over its ability to fend off the undead, what good would it do against the brute-ish entity in the hallway?

She waited and waited, for something to burst through and descend upon her to tear her apart and rob her of innocence in one fell swoop. She pressed her eyes and held her breath as those claws snagged on wood—and waited.

And then all fell silent, abrupt as death. The quiet rang in her ears.

Jane strained to listen for any signs of the intruder past the hammering of her pulse, but there was nothing. No scratching or groaning, as if whatever was on the other side simply vanished.

Knife pressed against her cheek, Jane choked every breath and whimper that threatened to squirm up her throat. But she kept silent, and listened, and waited.

And waited.

CHAPTER

Six

HEN JANE'S EYES NEXT OPENED, GRAY LIGHT AND the smell of fresh coffee seeped through the sheets.

Realizing that someone had been in her room, she bolted upright and tore aside the covers. Her nightdress was unmarked, bearing no stains of tears or blood, and her skin was free of any damning blemishes, but she couldn't shake herself free of the sensation of claws against her bones, and her skin cradled between pointed teeth. She must've dreamt of wolves and beasts.

She sighed and rubbed her face in the palm of her hand, over the raw and pink impression the pin-knife left in her cheek, then ran her fingers through her hair. Perhaps it had all been a nightmare.

She took the coffee, smelled it, and wrinkled her nose at its strong odor and the lack of cream. It was bitter in her mouth when she took a sip and she tried her best to not gag. She needed this, she scolded herself as she bit into a piece of buttered bread. She needed this to distance herself from last night's lingering dread.

Perhaps it had all been a nightmare, she thought—no, *hoped*—once more. But as she looked toward the bedroom door, left slightly ajar by whoever brought in the coffee and toast, the chewed clump of bread caught in her throat, but she was too afraid to choke.

Along the width of the threshold, scarring the floor, baseboards, and door with crooked fissures, were scratch marks. Ones that were very real and very deep, and snarling at Jane with teeth made of splinters.

⊤⊤ı⊤ıı⊤ıı⊤⊤ıı⊤⊤

MRS. FOSTER HAD LAID OUT A FRESH DRESS IN THE WASH-room for Jane. It was threadbare and its pink color was faded. It smelled like dust and sadness. Its puffed sleeves were loose around the shoulders and its too-short skirt exposed the ankles of the boots Jane stuffed her feet into. Mud still caked them, but was that not what a hearty set of boots was for? Still, Jane curled her lip at the mud. She hated having her things stained, just as she hated to go a day without her face powdered, lips painted, and eyes lined. Even her hair already began to adopt a bristling untidiness, with dark-colored tresses pointing every which way without her rose oil tincture to tame them. On her chin was a ruddy blemish and beneath her eyes were bags bruised by exhaustion, and it made her skin itch to not have such imperfections covered. She felt dirty, naked, exposed, as she trodded her way downstairs with her too-short dress, too-dirty boots, and too-bare face.

Jane found Mrs. Foster and Ms. Hudson chittering in the sitting room. They both fell silent when a floorboard creaked beneath Jane's step.

With the stuffy silence that hung between the three of them as Jane pulled her arms into her coat, she knew they, too, were aware of the scarred wood.

"Rest well, Miss Sterling?" Mrs. Foster asked in a hitched chirp. She wore a taut smile.

What are those scratch marks? What was that thing at my door? Why did you do nothing to wake me? The questions were at the tip of Jane's tongue, but they remained caged behind her teeth.

Neither of them bothered to wake her to inform her of the scratches or ask if she was all right. Neither of them brought up the marks with their words, but the creases at the corners of their mouths told her enough. They knew.

If they were playing coy now, she doubted they'd answer her questions.

She summoned her own tight smile. "Fine," was all she said before she put her head down and hurried outside.

The rain had stopped but it didn't take her walking far from the front door to see, even through the heavy fog, that the marshes were flooded. Almost to the point where the knoll upon which the Drowning House was situated had become its own little island. Only the back half of the carriage from the night before rose from the water a yard or two from the newly made shoreline, a sunken corpse.

She roamed the perimeter of the new 'island,' walking as close to the water as she could before mud tried sucking her down. She sank to nearly her knee with one step, muttering a curse under her breath. When she poised to free herself, balance was lost and she slipped. Her hands braced outward to stop her fall. Mud splattered across her cheek with a wet *smack*. The muck was seeping into her every pore and crevice, beneath her nails and between her toes, and she groaned.

"Damn mud and dirt and grime and—" she snarled, but stopped

as words caught in her mouth. Her one hand, swallowed past the wrist, had landed right in the center of a massive print, one with four toes and the indentations of four claws that mud seemed to undulate around. A shape like that of a paw, monstrous and large.

Mud gave a starved slurp as she pulled her hand free. She looked further down the waterline where there was another track. And then another, and another, until a trail ran along the water's edge.

The tracks were distinctly animal, but what kind of animal Jane couldn't tell, only that it was something large, something with claws.

It was a paw print like that of a wolf's, she noted, only... strange—it looked *wrong*. The space between the toes and metacarpal pads was too far, at least when compared to the tracks of other canids she'd observed on excursions with her father, and she identified the outline of what may have been the heel of a palm.

The track dwarfed the hand she held alongside it, nearly double the size. Recalling the claw marks on the door, she retracted her hand and balled it into a fist. She looked back out over the flooded marshes, wondering where such a thing would have come from— and where it could have gone.

"If not a bear, or a mountain lion, or a wolf..." As she mused aloud, she gnawed her bottom lip between her teeth. "Then what?"

England wasn't meant to have such beasts, not anymore, either due to the ways of nature or the persecution of man. If it weren't so damp she'd try to make a plaster mold of the print to bring home with her, maybe bring it to a museum to see what breed of specimen it was, if it were, or ever was, a known living creature. She was at least certain that the creature was mammalian, as she couldn't find impressions hinting at scales or feathers. Maybe she had just stumbled across a new species of animal, one with claws and a proclivity of scratching at the bedroom doors of young girls.

Did this animal also make a habit of hiding underneath beds and in the depths of wardrobes like some sort of boogeyman?

Maybe it wouldn't hurt for Jane to check under the bed. That was if she was to spend another night in the Drowning House. As she stared out into the flooded marsh, she begrudgingly accepted that she needed to consider that possibility.

Eager to put distance between herself and the bestial tracks, Jane stepped away from the water and started to trudge up the hill back toward the house. She hugged her arms around her as another breeze howled across the lawn.

Leaves scattered across the grass, having crept from the gray, moldered trees towering along the backside of the property. Requiring a distraction, enrichment, and evidence that could offer her hints at the strange animal's identity, Jane wandered toward them.

Her steps faltered as she neared the waterlogged border of the forest (if it could even be called such) for hidden in its shadows were several headstones. They were tall and elegant stone carvings, the tallest of which being an angel with its arms and wings stretched upwards whilst the shortest was an angel weeping atop its moss-laden plinth in mournful prayer. Four smaller stones, too thickly layered with rot and lichen to have their names read, surrounded the two main graves in a circular arch. A grim faerie ring, enticing Jane into its center to dance among the dead, just as the creature seemingly did the night before, as more of those monstrous tracks wove between the graves. Had it been a scavenger, seeking its next meal? Were these the tracks of a thing on the hunt or mad with boredom?

Tightening her coat around her, Jane took a step back, away from the meek cemetery. If it weren't for the very tangible, very savage marks on her bedroom door, she may have joked that the grounds were haunted by the black shuck she'd learned of during her London holiday.

Ravens cawing their throaty incantations drew her attention back to the trees. After a final glance at the graves, making note to ask Terence about them, along with the footprints, she turned to approach the woods.

And she almost wished she just returned to the house instead, for the woods were only a pathetic tangle of brambles, birch trees, and brown-hued despair that never once knew a day of life. Dead leaves and other autumnal debris littered land that steeped into a ravine, which seemed to be full of more muck. She curled her lip at it all. As she peered deeper between the trees and into the ravine, she saw something stark white protruding from the ground, something with the arched shape of what may have been a rib or an antler.

Ravens, one by one, took turns to swoop down and snatch morsels from the forest floor near the jutting growth. She couldn't see what they were plucking at through the foliage. Their warbles echoed through the trees like witches' laughter.

Jane wondered if the creature's den was somewhere in these shallow woods. Beasts and ravens shared a symbiotic relationship, omens of death drawn to one another for nourishment and survival. Despite the curiosity that ached in her ribs, she couldn't bring herself to take a single step into the woods. The trees stood crookedly, challenging her to walk amongst them in search of her mysterious beast. The swirls across their pale bark resembled eyes.

A shout from the house broke the trees' provoking stare, and Jane turned to see Terence crossing the lawn toward her with a powerful stride.

Several of the birds screamed and took flight upon his approach.

He was well-groomed and wore the heavy scent of cologne, but no amount of shaving and arranging hair could mask the weariness etched into the depths of his face. His eyes were rimmed with red exhaustion as he tried to muster a smile, and his dark tweed coat was draped across his forearm.

He stopped in his tracks just a foot away and pushed out a small laugh.

It was then when Jane supposed she must have resembled some sort of bog-pixie with her wind-tossed, short hair and face freckled with mud. Her nose wrinkled with a scowl.

"That's enough—" she grumbled as she scrubbed at her cheek with the back of her hand and flicked the dirt in his direction.

Like pouring water on a fire, his laughter died, but he failed to hide a restrained grin as he held up his coat. "In case you require further warmth. And—" his eyes traced the splattering of dirt and earth that painted the length of her body "—I can have another bath drawn for you if you'd like."

She didn't stop him from draping the coat across her shoulders, and her cheeks flushed when he brushed mud from her hair.

"Thank you," she mumbled, wrapping herself tightly in it. It smelled like him, with his scent of rain, bergamot, and lemon oil. She found herself leaning into it with a grateful sigh. "I didn't anticipate it being so cold. I may be a midwestern girl at heart but I'm not bred well enough to withstand such... dreary conditions."

"It must be that midwest blood of yours that drew you to the woods, then? Is it true that your part of America has deep, vast woodland? I've heard of the timber industry there, in the north, but was unsure of how true the stories were."

"Not as much now as a century ago, but yes, there are much and many trees. They say that before Europeans came, a squirrel could traverse from one side of the state to the other without ever touching the ground," Jane said, allowing his conversation to distract her from the bone-shaped thing she'd seen in the woods— the horrible paw prints along the water, the depressions between the graves, the claw marks on her door. "I must say, though, I've never been too enthused by your English forests. They always seem so... grim. Cold. Back home, I felt like I had company in the woods. Here, I only feel like I'm being watched. We certainly don't have creatures that leave paw prints like *that*." Using the toe of her boot, she gestured to the tracks circling the cemetery.

Beside her, she *felt* Terence go utterly still.

"Jane..." he started.

"I found more along the water, and I think whatever did this clawed up the guest room door something fierce. I was hoping you could tell me—"

"Y-Your door, Jane?" Terence's voice adopted a croaking shudder as a sallow pallor crept into his cheeks. He looked as though he would vomit.

She nodded. "I was afraid whatever it was—whether it be some dog or a fox—would break in and—"

"Your door—show it to me, please."

† †† ·† † ††· † ·†· † † †· ·†† †

WHEN JANE BROUGHT HIM TO THE GUEST ROOM DOOR, HER stomach dropped as Terence appeared even paler, more sick, with his mouth drawn into a tight line and eyes narrowed in a way that hinted at fighting down tears. He was as still as he was silent, save for his throat bobbing with a harsh swallow.

It was not the composure she wanted him to have. Despite the timidness of his nature, he was a big man who seemed like he was supposed to be unafraid of anything. To see him slack-jawed and shivering at splintered wood curdled something in her otherwise hollowed gut. How was she supposed to fling herself into his arms for protection if he seemed more frightened than she was?

"I wasn't sure as to what may have caused this," Jane cleared her throat. "I was thinking that an animal must've broken in, to shelter from the rain. A raccoon, maybe, or perhaps some sort of fox—"

His hand shook as he held it up to the fissures carved into the floorboards, his fingers curling into the shapes of claws seemingly out of instinct before he pulled back with a seething whimper. The same hand raked through his hair and he released a ragged breath.

In that moment, Jane decided she didn't like seeing his hair rumpled, and she refrained from reaching forward to rearrange the dark-and-silver strands that'd fallen into his face.

Instead, she tentatively cleared her throat and she started again, "See, I was just wondering if you or the staff had a dog because—"

He suddenly seized her by the shoulders, rousing a yelp out of her. "Jane, I... I am sorry."

The distress in his eyes bordered on insanity.

She winced. When she tried to shake from his grip, it failed to yield. "What for? This isn't *my* door—"

He continued with another gasp that rattled between his teeth, "I have tried my hardest to keep you safe from it, but there is an evil in this house I've no control over, and now it seeks to haunt us both."

Seven

JANE DIDN'T KNOW WHAT TO MAKE OF WHAT TERENCE had said, but she knew it left her ill at ease. So much so that she struggled to focus on—well, anything, as she already identified Terence's fossils to the best of her abilities. Her mind was but a slurry of thoughts and indistinguishable emotions as she worried a thumb over her trilobite locket.

She didn't have a chance to ask him what he meant because before she could even open her mouth to form words he released her and retreated to some other part of the house, leaving her to stand alone in the hallway, mouth hanging open, until Mrs. Foster came to insist that she bathe away the crusted mud.

After her bath and another change in wardrobe (which was another faded dress with a tail of pleated fabric running down her backside), and after Terence finally emerged from his hiding spot an hour or so later, they joined one another in the sitting room.

Jane tried to keep busy at the desk, mindlessly tapping at the fossils with the tip of a pen while the other hand pressed its thumb against the trilobite, memorizing the ridges of its ancient exoskeleton.

Terence had started a cylinder of music on the phonograph (some piano suite he never declared the title of) and was reading in his armchair, as if he hadn't just maddeningly informed her that they were, supposedly, haunted. But even then Jane could tell that the Terence who was now in her company was different from the one who greeted her so warmly on the lawn. She saw it in the stillness of his eyes as he pretended to read, the worried lines between his brow, the disarrangement of his hair, the newfound frumpiness in his collar, the tremor of his hands, the bouncing of his knee. Her stomach knotted at the scene, and she didn't know what she could say to ease tension for either of them.

As Jane looked at the fossils, the nub of her pen tracing the scale-like imprint of *Lepidodendron*'s bark, all she thought about were the claw marks. The patterns in the wood of the desk beneath her resembled their shape. She squeezed her eyes shut when she thought too much of what beast may have been pounding at her door—and stalking the grounds. And where it may have been hiding.

As she tried to imagine what breed of animal—real or something of myth—was capable of leaving such marks and striking fear into the heart of a grown man, she failed in her endeavor and decided to assign it the shadowy visage of a boogeyman, one with claws and pointed, interlocking teeth—perhaps not too unlike like the hooded figurine atop the fireplace mantle.

Jane tore her gaze away from the desk to look up at the idol. Through its veil, it watched her—somehow—and her bones tingled.

"How does one come into possession of such an ugly little doll?" She did little to tame the sneer in her tone.

"Doll?" Terence frowned before looking from Jane to the idol. He rolled his eyes. "Oh, *that* thing."

The exasperated "*that thing*" hinted at a story begging to be heard, and Jane gave an expectant raise of her brow.

"It's nothing too special. It was a relic of my grandfather's," he said.

Jane perked. "Was he an archaeologist or some such?"

He scoffed and looked down at his book as if he were going to pretend to read from it again. "If by 'some such' you mean 'daft', then yes, absolutely."

He rose and crossed the room to the bookshelf beside the desk where he grabbed something from a higher shelf and offered it to Jane.

She took the sepia-toned photo, held in glass and a simple silver frame. What she saw was a large family: a mother, father, three boys, and a young girl gathered around an old man with grizzled mutton chops sitting in the very center of them all. The old man's eyes were blurred, as though they'd been rapidly looking about whilst the photo was being developed, and a scar bubbled across the right hand curled in his lap. Everyone in the photo appeared weary, with sunken eyes and mouths prematurely lined. Disfigured shadows loomed over their shoulders, jagged and pointed, like wolves lurking somewhere behind them, waiting to pounce, but Jane assumed it was an illusion caused by the photo developing poorly, some disorganized set piece, or the rumpled state of the subjects' clothes.

The youngest of the children, standing between an exhausted mother and an even more exhausted father, stared at Jane with drooping eyes shadowed by a morose brow, and she smiled. Unlike his siblings and father, his hair was as dark as his mother's.

"So you've always looked like a kicked puppy, huh," she giggled.

He took the photo from her with a blush and clearing of his

throat. "I've only ever seen my grandfather twice in my life," he said quickly, an obvious distraction. "Once when this photo was taken, and again when he was in the grave."

Jane's smile fell. The cemetery in the yard. Was the rest of the family buried there, too? How many in the photograph lay beneath dirt trodden upon by nighttime beasts? She couldn't imagine the locals of Wolf's Run letting the Hayes bury their dead in the local graveyard if the glares they gave Terence's carriage were anything to go by.

"It was not much of a loss," Terence returned the photo to the topmost shelf, nearly hiding it from her view. "He never left his room, at least of his own volition—it was turned into the guest suite after he died. Mother said it was because he was afraid of something, and I've suspected that he was afraid of—" he tapped the idol and his hand jerked back as though it was stung, "—*this*. And his affinity for learning of the whims of spirits."

How comforting, Jane shuddered at the thought of sharing sheets that may have once held an old, dying man.

"He was a madman," he continued as he ran a knuckle over the books on the shelf, one of which simply read *Communications From Angels* in gold lettering on its spine. The ones beside it, *A Defence of Modern Spiritualism* and *Psychomancy: Spirit-rappings and Table-tippings Exposed*. "His love was with the occult, and my father told me he had attempted to dabble in Spiritualism but, supposedly, a spirit possessed my grandmother during a seance and twisted each of her organs one by one until she was sputtering so much blood attendees could no longer see their reflections in the waxed table and candles were extinguished—and then she *died*."

He lunged at Jane then, raising fingers curled into claws and teeth bared in laughter. She screamed and jumped backward until she fell out of her chair and hit the floor with a harsh thud.

"My apologies, I only jest," he said with a breathy laugh still softening his lips. "It was a stroke that killed her, in her sleep."

Out of instinct, Jane slapped the hand he offered, muttering a slew of curses under her breath as she got back to her feet.

"The statue was a totem he's had since before I was born, bought from some traveling merchants or peddlers or loons in London ages ago," Terence continued. The glow that had previously been in his eyes diminished the moment he looked back up at the idol. A droplet of sweat slithered down his neck. "I've never liked it. It feels as though it's always watching—and *knowing*."

"Ah, so he was an enjoyer of strange toys and outdated party tricks," she glared at the idol. In a way, she supposed it reminded her of animal-headed deities from Egypt—namely their death god, Anubis. Only this was ugly in the power it exuded, not grand like a deity warranting respect. She looked a little higher up on the wall above the fireplace and her disgust for the toy fizzled until it was replaced with a familiar thrill. "Was he a hunter as well?"

She approached the fireplace, reached up, and removed from its oak mount a hunting rifle. It nestled in her palms with a cool familiarity and an even cooler weight. "A Model 1895?"

Her thumbs brushed over thick grooves etched into the barrel in white scars; bullets gleamed from the mount like gilded teeth, eager to rupture through flesh.

"Only Ruben hunts, though not as much as of late—the rifle was one of his prized possessions. He had been saving for—goodness, I want to say *years*, to get himself a Winchester before I offered to purchase one for him. It's simply a decoration, now," Terence said, low and quiet, as he returned to his chair. "I would not know its precise model—your guess is as good as mine. How could you tell?"

Jane allowed herself to smirk. "I am an American. My blood

runs with bullets and my heartbeat is a gunshot." She then felt compelled to add, upon Terence's lack of immediate amusement, "My father hunts, on occasion. Not as much now, now that he's older, but still. Winchesters were his favorite, but more for decor, rather than to actively hunt with. He happens to have an 1895 mounted in his study."

She returned the rifle to its mount, careful to not brush against the idol while doing so. The cold imprint of the gun echoed in her palms, like the blood of a woodsman's gut pile abandoned in winter.

"Is that so?" Terence cocked his head and closed the book in his lap, using a finger to keep his page as he balanced it upon his knee. She was relieved that he didn't seem *too* bereaved at the mention of 'hunting.' That saddened crease pinched at the corners of his eyes. "I never took Dr. Sterling to be a hunter."

"Oh, one would think," Jane said. "He looks to be the hunting type, and his study resembles a gaming lodge. There must be dozens of mounted stag heads in there, and I know he at least has one elk mount, from when he went on a hunting trip out in Montana some handful of years ago." She used her hands to mimic the sprawling antlers of the elk, arched highly and pointed dangerously. For a moment she wondered if the beast at her door was scratching with antlers rather than claws, and she couldn't decide if such an image was more or less nightmarish.

"Would you hunt with him? Or your sisters? You'd sisters, correct? Or am I remembering things incorrectly?"

"*I* would—or rather I was his accessory while hunting. The idea of killing something was a notion I couldn't agree with, but I liked being out in the woods, and he would let me dig around leaves with him to look for animal bones or lost antlers," she let herself smile at the memory, at the recollection of her girlish hands burrowing beneath leaves slick with damp to scavenge the bones of a mouse from an owl pellet. "Meredith and Emmy were too busy being mother's prodigies to join hunts. But they're artistic, they're cultured—they're *proper*."

Terence tilted his head the other way. "I find you to be quite proper as well, Jane. In your own way."

In your own way.

Jane intended to smile but her lip curled into a scoff and her eyes rolled.

"Not always. Being the little heathen with dirt staining my skirts was my duty. It compensated, I think. My sisters, still, possess talents I do not. I could never sit still enough or conjure the attention to learn instruments or singing or painting or dancing as they did. All... *this*—" she gestured to all of herself, her cropped hair, the earrings she still wore. His gaze burned into her, truly *seeing* her, and she began to worry that with her lack of makeup he was observing a bit of mud she failed to wash away or a blemish blossoming in the crevice of her chin. So, she covered her chin, pretending to rest it in her palm, "—is compensation."

Terence was quiet for a moment as he sucked in a part of his cheek between his teeth. Perhaps he was trying to understand what she said, and a part of her envied that a man couldn't understand that particular ache of failing to fit into the role of the smart, cultured, high-society lady assigned to her, so much so that she felt it necessary to instead make herself into a doll who seemingly lacked a proper brain, just so that she could capture a fraction of the adoration her sisters received.

His lips twitched, toying with the syllables of 'compensation.' Jane was tempted to continue explaining how she hid her loneliness behind lace and laughter and dresses and boisterous words, but she pursed her lips to keep such temptation trapped. Perhaps he *could* understand such loneliness.

Terence was... different, compared to most men. He carried with him a lonely air.

"Do your sisters share a fondness for paleontology?" He asked once he decided to quit fondling silent words between his lips.

Jane couldn't resist a cackle at his question. "Oh, Christ, no! Meredith is too focused on being a musical prodigy and singing her heart out, and, when she isn't with her girls, Emmy spends too much time beneath the spotlight, on the tips of her ballet slippers, to care," she could sense something in her tone growing venomous the longer she spoke, but she didn't mind. Rarely could she voice her envy to someone who, at least as far as she knew, wasn't infatuated with her sisters. "They don't care about bones in the dirt. *I*, however, love them. I see a lot of myself in them."

At least none of us are self-proclaimed Spiritualists holding our-selves up in our rooms to be in the company of spooks and spirits.

Terence sank deeper into his seat with a sigh before folding his broad hands together and pressing his knuckles against his lips. He watched her with a ruminating stare. "And how is that?"

"It's the swift assuredness that we apply a label to things, to our-selves," she looked at the fossils on the desk and the small pieces of parchment she'd written their identities upon. "The constant bickering over who or what something is meant to be versus what they truly are until you no longer know who you are."

In a way, in my circumstance, it is a debate of my own design and a silent torture I have unknowingly crafted for myself, but I mustn't let you know that.

Terence hummed again. He narrowed his eyes, speculative but not incredulous. Once more, the corners of his eyes pinched, and that sorrow she'd felt at the greenhouse, which seemed to be half a lifetime ago, returned.

"At the same time I feel a great envy," Jane added and toyed with her locket. "Emmy, Meredith, Mother, Father... they all have their labels, but they're good labels one can admire. They can be remembered for staying true to a woman's image of being genteel and artistic and dignified, or a man of science and wealth. But I fall in the middle and..."—*And I try to not let it fester, though I can't help but feel a discomfort in the awareness of what I lack that makes them desirable, that I must dress loudly and speak my mind freely if I am to have any attention, good or bad*— "... every day I'm reminded that I'm not my sisters, and I know not whether to feel joy or sorrow for that."

Jane was certain her innards were spilling out onto the floor now as she held Terence's stare. In a sense, she was sure he would have his guts exposed, too. She'd never shared such feelings with anyone before. Insecurities have been her burden to bear, though only when she was sure no one was looking. But if Terence shared his own family secrets, why not share one of her own?

Quid pro quo, she thought, and as the silence lingered she held her chin up higher.

Terence's voice rumbled through the quiet as he shifted again in his armchair.

"I rather enjoy your company as is. You are a rare breed, Jane," he said, so soft and so gentle that she forgot to breathe. He added in a whisper that brushed against her ears like a kiss, "And I wouldn't have it any other way."

Eight

FOR THE FIRST TIME SINCE SHE WAS A SMALL CHILD, Jane decided that she wouldn't get a lick of rest until she checked for monsters under her bed.

Whatever oppressive air that had nestled itself between the house's every brick, every floorboard, every window pane, turned the blue of the guest room even bluer, the dust-tinged air even dustier, and the rain against the windows even rainier. And Jane wasn't fond of any of it.

Another grumble of thunder reverberated beneath Jane's knees as she placed the oil lamp beside her on the floor; the pin-knife was gripped in a fist. Though she knew there wouldn't be any sort of beast beneath the bed, a boogeyman crafted out of shadows and fear, she just needed to be sure...

The ruination of her door, the tracks in the mud, the prickling anxiety, punctuated by an even more uneasy silence, and everybody's ignorance of whatever was wrong with the house pressed upon Jane's shoulders in a discomforting weight.

Something was wrong, she was sure of it. If not wrong, then at least *off*.

The stories of Terence's grandfather—Jane had taken to calling him "Old Man Hayes," for he felt too much like a morbid rumination to be given a name, or even some familial term of endearment—only made her feel even more ill at ease. Checking under the bed was the least she could do to ensure that no intruder or wild animal managed to sneak his way in during the day.

Jane knew the only animal she could possibly find under there would be dust bunnies, yet something cool roiled in her belly, telling her to crawl into bed and turn a blind eye, and wait for the safety of daylight so that Mrs. Foster could take on the responsibility instead. Then again... if Jane *didn't* check, that part of her brain that remained like that of an animal, hellbent on survival, would nag at her like a disgruntled grandmother until she'd give into its whims and look anyway.

The floorboards were cold beneath her as she lay down on her belly. She had been holding her breath and only dared to let it go when she, at last, saw the entirety of underneath the bed—in all its empty glory, awash in the lamp's dim yellow glow. No eyes glowing red, no slobbering teeth waiting to gobble her up, no hands reaching to defile her. Only crooked shadows that ran along the lengths of the boards. Heat flooded her cheeks and she huffed out a small laugh that then rolled into a disappointed grumble.

"Christ, Janet... You're no child, letting your imagination run wildly like that—" she growled under her breath as she started to rise, but as she took the lamp in hand, she noticed its light snag peculiarly across the floor. The lines she saw were not straight and uniform in a way that would hint at natural patterns or wear in the wood, but rather in shapes that were arched and curved in too-complex designs. Had there been even more scratches from the thing that'd assaulted her door?

Bringing the lamp with her as far as she could without catching her sheets aflame, Jane flopped back onto her belly to scoot her way beneath the bed. Dust wavered around her in a golden haze and she bit her lip in an attempt to fight against a rising sneeze, especially as she narrowed her eyes to better understand what she was now looking at.

There were carvings, many of them. Some of them were maddened, nonsensical scratches, as if the carver made a mistake and attempted to claw it out of existence, while others were clearer patterns Jane traced with her pinky. Horseshoes, crosses, large, unblinking eyes with runes in place of a pupil. The most prevalent were looping, wheel-like patterns resembling flowers with six petals.

Jane was unsure of what to feel: fear in knowing this was hidden beneath her the whole time, a battling confusion and curiosity as to why Old Man Hayes—as she couldn't think of anyone else doing so—would make such carvings.

She shimmied back out from under the bed, reached into her bag for a sheaf of parchment and a piece of charcoal, and returned to lay amongst the dust with a new sense of excitement sparking in her heart. With her own scribbles, she started to trace the carvings.

Again and again, she drew horseshoes and evil eyes until a small stack of drawings piled beside the lamp. If her door weren't locked and if she weren't so scared to see those scratches scarring the threshold, she'd sneak down to the sitting room to retrieve one of Old Man Hayes' books to decipher the markings—and perhaps figure out why they were under the bed. It'd be a new assignment for her, now that Terence's fossils had been, for the most part, identified, and, hopefully, one to rescue her from another day riddled with apprehension and boredom—and pouring her deepest feelings of inadequacy to a man she'd only known for days.

Just as a triumphant heat swelled between Jane's breasts, a scream echoed outside her window. She jumped at the sound, causing the bed to shake when she hit her head against its metal frame. She seethed as pain ebbed in her rattling teeth.

Another drone of thunder snarled against the window until it melted and gave way to a howl, one that came from a mouth, not the sky. It was haunting, shrill, too much like that of a human scream than the bray of a wild beast.

It struck Jane deep in her chest, with emotions reminding her of the thing that'd scratched at her door: Terror. Dread. Horror. But also a deep, unmoving curiosity.

Emboldened by the fact the howls echoed from outside in the rain rather than outside her bedroom door, Jane scuttled from beneath the bed and staggered to her feet. Dust painted the front of her night dress, charcoal stained her fingers. The floor was bitingly cold, and she held her excess skirt in one great fist as she took small, cautious steps toward the window. Her breath fogged the glass when she peered into the night swollen with rain and thunder.

That was when she saw *it*—just a great, dark mass that moved along the distant treeline, but Jane knew it to be the animal, she was sure of it! What else could it have been, other than some apparition crafted from darkness playing on wavering reeds and shrubbery?

A flash of lightning illuminated its sheer size, and Jane stumbled back from the window with a gasp. It was a large animal. Too large for her comfort. It was the size of a horse, if not bigger, with a bulk like that of a bear. Even from a distance, she saw its eyes glowing yellow. Was the forest even capable of hiding an animal of that size during the day? Perhaps it was another poor creature stranded in the marshland by the floods, just as she and the staff were. But why or how would it end up inside the house to claw at her door? What kind of animal of that size would even be roaming English marshes, unable to swim and so afraid—if not incompetent—that it allowed itself to remain trapped? She wasn't sure if she wanted to explore and find out, not yet, anyway. That courage was reserved for daytime hours, and daytime hours only.

Jane stared intently, not daring to blink as the shape lumbered into the shadows of the trees, and from their depths rang another screaming howl, like the echoing moan of a man, lost, afraid—and hungry.

Nine

MISTLETOE WAS DEAD.

Near the stables, in a distant, waterlogged corner of the property, everyone stood around the horse's carcass when Jane crossed the lawn to join them. She had seen them from the guest room window, and it wasn't until she was washed over by the coppery reek of blood that she realized what they were gathered around.

As she approached them, she kept a wary eye on the woods—and the fresh tracks that now marked its border. She couldn't see yellow eyes watching her, only the ravens.

Mrs. Foster was crossing herself, Ms. Hudson held a palm to her mouth to hide quivering lips, and Ruben wept as he knelt beside the horse, blubbering something Jane's ears couldn't work out through the discordant sounds of his grief. Terence had been standing between them all, looking especially discontent and noticeably disheveled when Jane caught his attention.

His stride swallowed great lengths of earth as he came to meet her. "Look away, Jane! Please, go back to the house, *now*—"

He reached to grab her arm but she stepped back with a scowl. "What? You think of me too delicate to see blood—"

But it was too late. She caught a glimpse of the body and bile surged into the back of her throat.

The mare lay on her side, belly split open to reveal what remained of her organs—a mess of viscera, congealed blood, and entrails strung like pearls between broken ribs. Her throat bore a gaping hole, the wound ragged along its edges from being torn asunder by horrible teeth. The kill was older, not fresh enough to steam in the November chill and blood having long since moldered into a brownish maroon. It was a slaughter, one that frightened Jane so because this was not just the death of an animal typical of nature's cruelty. It was the intentional desecration of something tame, domestic, *civil*. A kill done for the sake of a killing, for the sake of channeling rage. Survival was not what occupied this beast's mind as its teeth ruined flesh. If the beast maimed a horse, how much longer until it sank its fangs into one of the staff, Terence—into *her*?

Taking her elbow, Terence whispered harshly, "*Jane*—inside with Lottie and Georgianna. Please." His words stumbled and his tone was tense as he hissed that final syllable.

Jane looked up at him with her own wordless plea, tongue paralyzed. His hazel eyes were a storm, winced and shadowed with a despair that'd begun to frighten her. "T-Terence—"

Before Jane could even have a moment to ask more about Mistletoe, Mrs. Foster swooped over and replaced Terence's touch on her arm to usher her back to the house.

"Y-yes—yes, come, Miss Sterling. It's gnarly, garish business, it is." Mrs. Foster's chatelaine jingled with every step, the sound shuddering as fiercely as her bony fingers that dug into Jane's arm.

Jane looked behind them as Terence tore a hand through his hair and returned to Ruben, still hunched over Mistletoe.

Blood ran deep in the mud, filling in another print right beside the body, a print in the shape of a beast's paw.

⸶⸸⸷⸶⸸⸷⸶⸸⸷⸶⸸⸷⸶⸸⸷

BACK IN THE HOUSE, MRS. FOSTER AND MS. HUDSON HAD taken to ignoring Jane to instead speak to each other in hushed, frantic whispers in the kitchen.

Under the guise of making tea, Jane tried to eavesdrop but as she waited for the kettle to boil, both women replaced their chittering with sharp sideways glances she couldn't read. Ms. Hudson's glare was indecipherable as she took Mrs. Foster by the arm and, together, rushed from the room to resume their whispering elsewhere.

Jane tried to ignore a bitter twinge within her. Why wouldn't they include her in such conversation, especially if it may have concerned whatever beast may have been roaming the grounds?

Still waiting on the kettle and requiring some semblance of movement in her numbed, tingling limbs, she retrieved her drawings from upstairs and ran a finger along Old Man Hayes' books in the sitting room until she pulled out the first title she thought would be of most use (and entertainment) to her—*On Wards Against Spooks, Demons, Witches, & Warlocks* by some unnamed author, and seemed to be more in the style of an old, flimsy, amateur penny dreadful than something of proper literature. She brought both to the conservatory, a room she'd only glimpsed out of the tail of her eye during previous wanderings of the house, as she decided she could use a change in scenery for the day's activities, having grown tired of the sight of stale, sad blue wallpaper.

Jane returned with her tea, which she wasn't even thirsty for, and plopped herself into one of several plump armchairs that occupied the room. The golden upholstery squealed beneath her slight weight and layers of ornately-patterned rugs pillowed her steps. The room was cozy, lit by several Tiffany lamps that cast a kaleidoscope of red and green shades across the bookshelves lining each of the four walls. A residual scent of cigar smoke, having long since seeped into the wood for eternity, hung faintly in the air like a ghost. Rain pinged against the domed skylight in a gentle symphony, creating a fragile serenity that felt in poor taste.

Jane wished she had said something about the beast she saw, that she suspected it of being Mistletoe's murderer. She winced, pressing her eyes shut as the image of the horse's maimed throat, the blood-soaked paw print beside it, burrowed its teeth into her brain. It wasn't until she went to take a sip from her tea and the ping of rattling porcelain started to ricochet off the skylight that she noticed her hands were shaking; her appetite was missing, her thirst nonexistent. The chamomile was a sludge on her tongue and she struggled to swallow as it clawed its way down into her belly like molten sandpaper.

She sighed and sat back in the chair so that she could watch the rain dribble across the skylight. She suddenly hated the rain. The more it rained, the longer she would be stuck at the Drowning House, deep in the bowels of the Wolf's Run marshes. No horse to ride or to pull a carriage meant she'd have to resort to walking to Wolf's Run to hail a cab back to Cambridge—that was if she wasn't so worried about ruining her wardrobe, on top of drowning in an ocean of mud.

Jane began to wonder how her mother was faring in her absence.

She wondered if anyone had told Mrs. Sterling about the rains flooding the marshes, and that there was a logical reason for her daughter to be gone, not because of a murder or being gobbled up by some marshland creature—

Jane smacked her palms against her thighs. She couldn't allow herself to stew in these thoughts for too long, for, in time, they'd score unpleasant lines along her mouth and sag below her eyes.

Turning to the book and pile of papers, she took her drawings and spread them across her lap, offering her a view of each one. After another sip of tea to moisten her cracked lips, she flicked through the thin book. She didn't pause to read any passages, instead seeking out symbols and illustrations that could hint at anything useful. Most pages had illustrations, some pentagrams and crescent moons—protection sigils if the title was anything to go off of—though none resembled her drawings.

Without her glasses, her eyes had grown sore with all their flickering between the book and her drawings, and she tossed the book onto her lap with an exasperated sigh. As she rubbed her temple with a thumb and forefinger, she found that she was pinned beneath the stare of a great, unblinking eye peering up at her from the page the book splayed open to. At the eye's center, in place of a pupil, was a spiraling, circular rune, not too unlike in Jane's drawings.

In the margins of the page were nonsensical scribblings, wavering lines of ink scratched into the paper with a slanted, etching script. The penmanship of Old Man Hayes?

Jane canted her head to the side and held the book up to her face so she could attempt to read without her glasses. Only managing to decipher every other word between her farsightedness and Old Man Hayes' poor handwriting, the annotations described the eye to be used as a general ward against evil, an "evil eye," a malevolent stare of envy and misfortune to frighten away spirits—the eye of a protective God. But what spirits was Old Man Hayes so afraid of that warranted, seemingly, several protective sigils carved into floorboards?

Jane's finger tapped the drawing of the eye. If this symbol was to ward off evil, then she was certain the others beneath the bed were as well. It was now only a matter of deciphering what Old Man Hayes felt he'd need protection against. She paused her tapping. Had he been seeking protection against the beast, something similar to the one clawing at her door, murdering horses, and skulking in the dark of night?

What if legends of the black shuck were true—

Jane scoffed and rolled her eyes. "*No*. It's nothing more than Spiritualism and spooks shenanigans—"

Lightning flashed, blinding the room, a heartbeat before it was pursued by a clap of thunder that shook the house and rattled the skylight panes.

Jane jumped with a yell. Her knee knocked against the table holding her tea, and she hissed as the thing shattered on the floor in an explosion of porcelain chips and hot liquid.

"Oh, that's just lovely..." she muttered, closing the book and setting it on the arm of the chair. Grumbling, she got down on her knees, created a little pocket with the excess fabric of her skirt, and started to gather the pieces of the chipped cup. As the tea soaked into the rug with a brownish stain and a heat that bled beneath her knees, she tried to ignore how much it reminded her of spilled blood, and the white chips she gathered like little teeth.

She reached for a particularly large, particularly jagged, piece that fell beneath one of the chairs when her finger caught on a frayed seam in the rug, causing its edge to flip back just enough to expose the floorboards underneath. Floorboards that, Jane noticed, possessed a funny crookedness, as if mislain whether on accident or with great haste to hide something. Atop the most crooked of the boards was the black smudge of singed wood.

She set her gathered pieces of broken cup on the table, then, with great effort heaved and pushed the armchair aside enough so that she could have a better view of the crooked floorboard. A sigil was rotted into the wood, another one of Old Man Hayes' evil eyes, surrounded by carvings of crosses. Terence's stories of his grandfather's inclination to dabble in the occult flooded back to her and rushed a thrill through her veins. Perhaps she had just stumbled across yet another one of the old man's occult secrets. She bit her bottom lip to tame her morbid giddy. With little hesitation, she jammed a prodding finger into a notch in the board and wriggled it loose.

She couldn't resist wheezing out a triumphant cackle when she pulled the square of floor up to reveal a hidden compartment—and the little book that was hidden inside. It'd felt like uncovering a treasure, one that she wasn't meant to find. She wished Mr. Thompson was here so she could share the excitement of her find as she picked the book up and turned it about in her hands. It was small, perhaps a journal or a pocket bible, bound in flimsy leather and tied closed with a piece of twine. Imprinted on its cover were more crosses.

She glanced at the conservatory door, listening for any approaching footsteps or conversation, and once she was sure she was alone, she undid the string and leafed through the pages, brittle and yellow at the edges beneath her fingers. Damp had gotten to the book, with a corner of its cover stained black with mold. The crust of old rot ruined the ink on most pages to the point they were hardly legible. Jane wrinkled her nose with disgust and wiped a hand against her skirt. Not so much a treasure but rather a piece of garbage that stank of age and left a grimy powder on her fingertips. She would've put the book back where she found it to then forget about it if it weren't for the crosses on the cover and a page soaked with violent sketches.

Abruptly, she stopped her sheafing and hurriedly flipped back to the page with the illustrations. At last, she found it and slammed a finger down to claim its place on the page.

The sketches were garish, yet Jane couldn't help but find a familiarity in them. The crude, scribbled angles hinted at them being drawn in some feverish vigor rather than artistic amusement. In a way, it reminded Jane of the drawings of malformed dinosaur skulls she'd claw into her mother's sketchbooks as a child. But these weren't the drawings of a child with daydreams. No, this was something else.

In the page's center, most prominent, was something resembling some canine skull, or at least Jane thought it to be so. A very ugly one, with a snout both too long and too broad, and eyes set too loose in otherwise hollowed sockets. Circling it in the same chicken scratch was a single word, written again and again, until it created an unholy halo around the skull: *CLAUNEK.*

Jane's nose wrinkled again. What was a "Claunek"? Was it a spell? An incantation, a hex? A name, a species? And what did it have to do with a poorly drawn dog's skull? Was that the name Old Man Hayes prescribed to the beast as though it were some pet? Jane could picture Old Man Hayes, bent and broken and crooked with age as he hunched over the book, carving that word onto paper just as he carved evil eyes on the guest room floor. Once more, she had to ask herself why and for what, and against whom.

Beneath the skull was another sketch that, upon first glance, almost resembled a blot of ink. But distinctly rough lines hinted at a vague shape of what could have been a dog—in the sense that it had a body, four limbs, bristling hair, and a yawning jaw full of teeth like a wild mongrel. There were two empty, unmarked voids that the drawing's body seemed to orbit. The eyes of a beast.

The eyes of a Claunek?

Jane lingered on the drawing, her fingertip lightly circling it until it turned black with the phantom remnants of ink. She imagined the thing's claws clotted with splinters and its mouth stained in blood as it snapped at the pulse in her throat—

Music flittered into the room and Jane jumped. She looked over her shoulder, half-expecting to see someone lurking in the doorway. But there was nobody, only the distant echo of thunder and the melancholy trill of a harpsichord. It began as something like a ghostly song, whispering and dull, but enough to keep her attention away from the moldy book in her hands. Had someone put a cylinder on the phonograph, to drown out the weighted sorrow in this house? The music was too clear, too organic, to be a cylinder.

Gingerly, she put the book back under the floor and replaced the loosened floorboard. She could return to the book of beasts and Clauneks later. She flipped the rug back over the spot and went to investigate the music, scrubbing her hands clean on her skirt as she went.

As she suspected, the music was someone playing the harpsi-chord in the sitting room, but she was surprised to see Terence seated at the instrument, his fingers caressing the reverse-colored keys with a grace she never thought him capable of having. There was no music before him, and his eyes were shut as he gently swayed to his own orchestrated rhythm.

There was a tranquility in the scene, and Jane leaned against the doorway and just took a moment to listen to him, silent. Her eyes traced the blunt aquiline lines of his profile, the way weariness grayed his features, the shadows deepening the lines around his mouth and eyes so that he appeared both troubled and content all at once. He'd the countenance of a musician, perhaps even a tortured poet. Whatever he was, Jane preferred it over the fear she saw earlier. He wore melancholy better than he did fear.

As his hymn slowed to what must have been its ending, Jane seized that moment to clap a muted applause.

Terence jumped in his seat and swiveled to stare at her. He must've been so entrenched in his music that he failed to notice he accumulated an audience of one.

"Oh, Jane," he stammered a bit, brushing his palms against his trousers as he scooted back on the bench in preparation to stand. "Forgive me if I interrupted something, I just—"

"Why apologize for something so lovely?" Jane strode across the room until she leaned against the harpsichord with her chin cradled upon the heel of her palm. "I never took you to be a man of music. Seems like you've been full of surprises, hm?"

Thankfully, Terence remained in his seat but his shoulders were rigid, nervous. "My mother was a very musical type. She ensured all of us boys learned an instrument, my father too."

"Is that so?"

With a timid jerk of his head, he gnawed on his lip. "I was the only one with passion for the skill." And he said no more.

Jane sensed he didn't wish to speak further on the subject, so she didn't press on it despite the insistent eagerness to do so. She let it be. Instead, she said, "Do you perform? You've the skill of a man who could draw numbers to music halls across the world, I'm sure. This could take you across all the known continents if you wished. It's a talent that should be shared." *Not kept caged in this sad house.*

Terence lightly traced his fingers over the keys before folding them together in his lap, shaking. His shoulders drooped beneath the weight of a sigh—and perhaps even more. "Please know that if I could, I would. I would love to share music with others. The truth is that I... I..." His eyes were cast toward the floor as he seemed to search for said truth before wetting his lips and looking to his lap, brow furrowed. "I've never traveled beyond Britain before. And I wish I were able to."

Jane leaned closer. "And why aren't you able to?" She asked, perhaps a little too eagerly as she bit her bottom lip with a grin.

She received no response beyond him mumbling something she thought to be, "You wouldn't understand," which she wanted to huff about, but she knew it was not her business to know, even if she liked to think she was entitled to such knowledge.

Sighing, she let the topic fall dead to the floor.

She then sat beside him on the bench and stifled the urge to smirk at how he tensed beside her.

"Teach me," she demanded, cool and blunt.

He cleared his throat. "I beg your pardon?"

"I'd like for you to show me how to play," She said, looking at him expectantly. "I'm a horrid student but I've nothing else to do as of right now." *Except learning a little more about your strange house and stranger family...* "I wouldn't want to die of boredom, now!"

When he looked at her, it was with an intense stare which smoldered his hazel eyes into a charred brown and the corner of his mouth wavered into the ghost of a smile, as if he was studying her. Not in a way that made her feel like an object, but rather a marvel. A warm sensation trickled through her chest and she sat up a little straighter.

"Y-Yes, of course. I am not one to teach, but I shall try my best, Jane," his mouth caressed the utterance of her name, and she wished to hear him say it again—and again, and again.

Instead, he held his hands over the keys, fingers splayed, poised, ready. He nodded to her own. "Place your hands over mine."

And she did, his hands hot and shaking beneath her palms. She blushed at seeing their hands together, at the tickling texture of his hair and raised veins. The heat from her chest entered the tips of her ears the more her mind began to wander—

He, slowly, began to play a melody. It was a familiar one, with the cadence of what felt like a child's lullaby, a nursery rhyme, the notes gentle staccatos. One that if someone didn't know it then perhaps they had a marred childhood—which worried Jane for she couldn't conjure a name for this particular tune. She couldn't name the tune, but she could *almost* name the sensation that made her heart ache with a desire to grieve.

"Something of my own composition, of sorts," his breath warmed the shell of her ear. "I allow whatever emotion troubling me to take hold of me and release itself across these keys until I am at ease."

Jane pressed into him. "And what emotion puppets us now, maestro?"

He gave no answer, and instead, she saw a wry smile strain his mouth as he continued with his refrain.

Together they played the same tune again and again, to a point where Jane was certain she could play it with her eyes closed.

Meredith would have loved Terence. She would've loved to find a way to play her cello in tune with his harpsichord and to turn such harmony into courtship. Jane didn't want to think of that, though, and banished it with a grit of her teeth. She wanted this one admirer, this one friend, to be solely hers—for once. The carnal urge to claim him urged Jane to scoot closer to him, to lean further into his warmth, to press her hands harder upon his. She needed him to be hers.

Hers.

There was a sudden chill beneath her fingers and a loss of a consistent tempo within the music that pulled her out of the haze of desire and possession. She broke free of the envy wriggling in the folds of her brain to see that she had become the musician. Terence's hands braced her elbows, the small of her back, to correct her posture.

"Very good," he whispered against her ear despite the discordant twang of Jane playing a wrong note.

She was playing music, not well or very elegantly, but it was music nonetheless, and her heart fluttered as his hand lingered against her back, burning through fabric and into her skin.

She hummed and twisted her mouth in a smirk. "Thank you."

As much as dread had turned her belly into lead and excitement frayed her nerves, she decided that, for now, she could forget about blood and murdered horses and hidden books and beasts, and instead fixated on the heat of his touch, his sigh that tickled her hair as he whispered with a grim breathlessness, "Beautiful, Jane."

⸸⸸⸸⸸⸸⸸⸸⸸⸸⸸⸸

SHE WASN'T SURE HOW, WHY, OR WHEN SHE CAME TO THIS conclusion, but Jane realized that she and Terence never shared a dinner together. They did have lunch together in Cambridge, yes, but never the formal dinner she would've expected having in an expensive Englishman's house. She had hoped for dinner at a table so long it could host an entire king's court and illuminated by glittering candelabras that dripped threads of wax all over the food, which would have been piled in mounds that'd make her mouth water. Mountains of turbot in lobster sauce, mutton cutlets, braised beef, and quail served on silver platters, crystal decanters of red wine gravy, soups ladled with gilded spoons. But the lack of such was a disappointment, much like how the Drowning House—this whole trip—had been a disappointment.

She couldn't help but resent that fact, and felt that Terence ought to have an obligation to dine with her as a guest—and perhaps even as a friend. Especially after several days and nights of a haunting steeped in blood.

Jane had it all planned out: they'd have dinner, then they'd dance in the sitting room (she already prepared to ask him, as she predicted he'd lacked the bravery to do so himself) when she'd then be seduced in his arms as they moved lazily in time to some flowery waltz he played on the phonograph, nevermind the fact she didn't dance. She imagined that Terence could. Beneath the timid quivering, he wielded the restrained elegance of a performer, a gentleman, a lover. She wondered how gentle his kisses would be, if his lips would shake shyly against hers and allow her to take the lead, or if he was an animal starved and depraved with want. She couldn't decide which she liked more. It was thoughts such as those, intoxicating in their sickly sweetness, that prompted her to abandon where she sat at the harpsichord, chasing the memory of how Terence's touches felt as his hands held her steady, and stepped into the kitchen.

Ms. Hudson hadn't set out to make dinner yet, and Jane hadn't seen her or Mrs. Foster or Ruben since the incident with Mistletoe that morning (she couldn't blame them for sequestering themselves to their quiet corners of the house for the time being), so she thought she could try to make... something herself. Jane wasn't by any means a cook, her skills being nothing more than what she learned from observing the cooks who toiled in her family's kitchen when she was a child, but she could at least put things and spices together to create a meal that could be somewhat edible. And one of those things she could make was soup.

With the kitchen to herself and a quiet having befallen upon the house, she rolled up her sleeves and set to work.

Her hands still felt the phantom sensation of Terence's beneath hers, the whispers of his melody continued to find a home in her ears, as she chopped potatoes and started a pot of water. Those lingerings had become an incessantly pleasant distraction, even long after he dismissed himself to his own corner of the house, seemingly for the evening, and left her in the sitting room, but not before reminding her to retire to bed—and lock her door—by nightfall. She elected to disobey that request, just this once, as she wasn't necessarily in a rush to return to the company of Old Man Hayes' carvings, not yet, at least.

Night encroached on the Drowning House, and Jane hoped that whatever made the house and its master and staff so afraid of it—whether it be the beast or something more foul—would seek her out only if it meant that Terence would come to her rescue, armed with the Winchester rifle, and press her flush against the heat of his bosom as he kept her safe, keeping evil at bay with his gentle, large, trembling hands—

She coughed and laughed as her cheeks grew warm.

"He is hardly the protecting type," she mused aloud with a smile. "I feel like it's more likely for me to protect him rather than him protecting me." She failed to find disappointment in that speculation, at least. In fact, she found it equally handsome.

What Jane ended up making was a simple potato soup. (She made a note to have Mrs. Sterling write a check for Ms. Hudson to compensate for the foods and tools Jane used.) A gentle aroma filled the air in the kitchen, and she was proud of herself—until she tasted her creation. It wasn't awful, just... bland. Too watery and too salty, with hardly any flavor aside from the hint of heavy cream. And it somehow tasted burnt.

She didn't care. Dinner, regardless of quality, was but another excuse to steal more of Terence's company for herself rather than being alone, stewing over beasts and Clauneks and wards against evil forces.

Just as she ladled the soup into bowls and turned to retrieve Terence from wherever he was hiding, she was startled to see that he was already lurking in the kitchen doorway.

Excitement sparked in her chest upon seeing him, but in that same instant, the spark snuffed itself into oblivion.

He was... changed. This wasn't the Terence she'd been with in the sitting room. This Terence stared at her with a malicious anxiety that rivaled the distress he wore that morning. His white shirt was unbuttoned to expose a heaving chest glistening with clammy damp. Hair hung loosely over a face carved with the harsh lines of fear, and his eyes were blown so wide open she saw the sleepless red that fringed them. Across his throat slashed a brutal scar, a collar of smoothed flesh. Jane nearly asked him about it.

He looked feral. Utterly primal and ravenous.

"You look as though you've seen a spook," Jane said, her smile nervous.

"You are not in your room," he said, and the bluntness of his observation made her laugh.

"Well, obviously. I thought you'd enjoy some dinner with me, and—"

"To your room, Jane. Now," he spoke past gritted teeth, and each word pushed through in a taut grunt. "*Please.*"

Her brows knitted together and her jaw hung loose as she searched for a reply. "But I thought we could—"

"*Jane*—" she flinched at the way he snarled her name horribly from somewhere in the back of his throat. "I beg of you. I will not argue this, I just—" He huffed as his hands clawed through his hair. She could practically hear the violent thrum of his heartbeat in his throat, and it resembled the roiling thunder outside.

Jane narrowed her eyes and raised her chin. *What's wrong? Is there something I can do to help?* "Why should I go to my room?"

The moment he bared his teeth and barked a sharp, "*Because I told you to*!" Jane wished she'd held her tongue.

He drew a long breath in through his nose in a faltering attempt at composure. "Because I am *begging* you to do so, Jane. I... J-just—listen to me, *please*, and *go*."

A dread not too unlike what fermented after his ominous warning following her first night at the Drowning House returned to spiderweb its way through Jane's gut, and her appetite—for both soup and company—dissipated. His breathing had become increasingly ragged, the hollows of his face deepened, his shoulders slouched as though he were a scolded dog when she glared at him, lips turned downward in a frown.

She didn't know what to feel in this moment as they held each other's gazes, the sweat on his brow leaking down his face like tears, but an emotion she could name was *hurt*. But she couldn't let such hurt show.

She curled her lip in a sneer before she carelessly dropped one of the bowls onto the counter. The bowl, to her chagrin, didn't shatter, but a mess of spilled cream and potatoes was made.

"Tomorrow, I expect answers for all—" with her free hand she gestured to, well, all of him, the house. Her fingers were bent to form claws. "Because I am tired of whatever games and mysteries are being played here. Goodnight, Mr. Hayes."

So she avoided his gaze as she took her bowl and went to her room.

Out of spite, she didn't bother to have her door locked.

CHAPTER

Ten

ANE STARTLED AS A BLOOD-CURDLING SCREAM TORE through the house.

A deathly silence followed, practically shaking the floorboards.

She froze beneath her sheets as another howl echoed against the pipes, rattling foundations so that it seemed as though it were the Drowning House that was crying in agony.

She waited for another sound, holding her breath, but heard nothing other than the rain, wind, and lightning that hissed against the windows.

Had it been the mystery animal? Did it break in and attack one of the staff? Or, and her gut curdled away whatever anger had remained there for him, did it get Terence? The sounds were too alive, too powered by torment, to be a mere settling of the house or even thunder. Whether it was Terence, the staff, or an animal, the sound was horrible, soaked in blood, and Jane needed to know how much blood. She knew she should've been more afraid, but that same, insistent nagging that'd wriggled into her brain when she'd discovered the carvings beneath the bed had returned with fervor.

Slowly, she cast her sheets aside and snatched the hairpin-knife, having never returned to its metallic sheath, from the nightstand. Beside it was her untouched bowl of cold soup. She didn't bother eating it, her appetite shot dead by the betrayal of Terence's outburst. Never would she admit it out loud but the callousness of his tone hurt. More than she anticipated. She never thought he, of all people, would raise his tone with her. It was what made her heart crack and her throat tighten as she'd pressed her back against her shut door, cries muffled into the heel of her palm.

She tried to read and she tried to sleep, but she instead bundled herself under the covers and stared at the rain smattering against the window, watching the flashes of lightning dance within the droplets, until the scream broke her out of her trance.

Her head still ached and her eyes remained blotched from her crying as she clutched the little knife, took hold of the oil lamp, held her breath, opened the door, and stepped into the hallway.

The silence that lay over the house was almost more grim than the screams that woke her. She was betrayed by every footfall as wood creaked beneath her toes. With every other step, she was compelled to look over her shoulder to ensure that Mrs. Foster hadn't burst into the hallway like a bat out of hell to drag her back into her room rather than assist her in investigating the screams. The thought hurried Jane's pace until she crept down the stairs and found herself in the kitchen, the gas lamp in her hand alighting everything beneath a yellowing, pestilence-colored hue. Though she wasn't near the sitting room, she couldn't shake the feeling of the idol's leer pulsing through her bones and settling at the base of her skull.

Holding her breath, Jane strained to listen for any sound that wasn't the din of the storm or her pulse hammering in her ears.

A groan assaulted the quiet, droning from behind a door Jane thought to be some sort of pantry, which now, beneath the light of her lamp, sat crookedly ajar. Damp air with the sweet, metallic odor of old, rotted meat wafted from the door, clearly not the scent of a pantry, but perhaps of an old cellar.

A sliver of blackness stared at her with the danger of a cat's eye, challenging her as another low groan rumbled from somewhere deep within.

Swallowing down the trepidation that started to scratch in her throat, Jane hoisted her oversized skirts higher in the same fist clutching her blade, eased open the door with her foot, and made her way into the darkness.

Stone stairs wound steeply downward, slick with a damp both natural and unnatural, and the walls glistened yellow beneath her lamp. The strong odor of discarded meat and rot was pungent in the air and assaulted every one of Jane's senses. Too much did this feel like being swallowed whole into the throat of a tomb, a crypt that hollowed out the earth beneath the Drowning House. Jane half expected to step down into a pit of bones that'd crumble and crunch beneath her weight as she reached the bottom-most step. Her toes met only with cold, wet stone.

She wrinkled her nose as the stench had become overpowering and her whole body shuddered with a gag. If she had eaten her soup from dinner, surely she would have certainly spewed sick all across the floor. A floor that Jane noticed to be marred by severe marks.

She crouched low and put a hand down to the scarred stones until her fingers snugly fit within four fissures running parallel to each other. Just as they did with the depressions beneath the entrance hall's wallpaper. And the splinters along the guest room door. She retracted her hand as though the stone burned her fingertips. These had to have been left behind by an animal, one very large, very powerful, very angry, as it clawed at the cellar floor, every inch of it it seemed.

It suddenly became difficult to breathe as Jane's heart lodged in her throat. Could this have been where Old Man Hayes' boogeyman-beast—his Claunek—was kept? Was this the resting place of the animal that was clawing doors, haunting the grounds, and murdering horses? If this were some animal or pet or boogeyman, what manner of creature was it that it'd driven a man to scribble madness into a notebook and carvings into his home?

"Wh-what *are* you…" she managed to whisper, and the darkness answered back.

Jane stopped breathing entirely as something shifted within the dark. There was the sound of something wet plopping against the stone floor.

In a shaking grip, she held the lamp higher, trying to see more of the cellar, before reeling backward until her back collided with the wall. A scream was trapped on the back of her tongue, too afraid to escape. She was surrounded by piles of rot. Rotted flesh, decayed meat—discarded and gathered in mounds in the cellar's dark corners, left to spoil. There were the rusted bits of many chains, many broken manacles, some scattering the floor, some partially lodged in the heaps of flesh, some hanging from loose bolts in the walls. It didn't matter. It all reeked.

A dungeon? A torture chamber?

Hell?

Jane's mind was scrambling to imagine this place's sickening purpose as she was assaulted by the sight of blood—so, so much blood—clumped in congealed puddles, streaked across the floor, painting the walls with hand-shaped prints. With a sickly, metallic sweetness, old blood was already seeping into her tongue, between her teeth, down her throat.

Despite her empty stomach, bile surged into her mouth and she gagged before swallowing it back down. It was the stench of spoiled blood and the thought that this hall of gore and horror had been lying beneath her feet without her knowing. And that Terence kept it a secret from her.

What had been kept down here? Who was bound with the bloody chains?

Some blood was still damp beneath her lamplight—someone had just bled.

She didn't have much time to puzzle through her terror any further as a slurp leaked out from the darkness. Something else was down here with her, and she didn't know what terrified her more: some*one* or some*thing*.

A beast? Old Man Hayes? Who? What?

Jane's head spun. She should have supposed that even the most kind-hearted of Englishmen would entomb a family member so that their embarrassment may remain in the dark. But what madness led to so much blood?

"Wh-Who's there?" She called out and a blunt blood-stained echo returned to her.

She held the lamp up again in an attempt to further illuminate the cellar, trying to peer past the mounds of flesh and manacles to focus on the hunched shadow in the furthest corner. Another wet crunch of bone or some other body part breaking resounded against the bloody stones.

She swallowed, licking her lips (and gathered her courage), and tried again, "Hello?"

The figure fell silent and went still, compelling Jane to cry, "Come now, who is that? I-I can see you!"

The figure shifted, a hulking dark mass that turned until two glowing orbs stared at Jane from the darkness. It sat before something glistening and damp—fresh gore, discarded flesh, and viscera.

Jane froze, her very heart going painfully still between her breasts, as the thing abandoned its mess of shredded clothes and blood and skin to stalk toward her. On all fours and hunched over like a wild animal. Gnashing teeth glittered with strings of freshly torn flesh. Pale claws scraped against stone. This was not Old Man Hayes, nor was it even remotely human. This was a nightmare.

Jane didn't know whether to weep, run, die, or fall to her knees before it.

The beast.

The beast's shape was something Jane could only describe as primal and prehistoric, uncanny in its mimicry of something mammalian with bowed, bear-like legs, square snout, and the yellow saber-shaped teeth its black lips peeled back to reveal. Down its back, piercing through sinewy gray flesh that stretched taut across a jutting skeleton, bristled a sparse covering of black and silver hair. Blood stained its jowls, the malformed protrusion of its muzzle, and bubbled at the corners of its mouth as it snarled again—and lunged forward, just as Jane screamed.

As she jumped back, the lamp slipped from her hands and plunged the room into darkness beneath the symphony of shattering glass and snuffed flames. There was the sound of fabric tearing as one of the beast's reaching claws snagged on the very edge of her skirt, nearly tripping her. Jane wrenched herself free by turning on her heel and clambering up the stairs on all fours in a blind scramble.

She didn't dare look behind her, instead focusing on the pinprick of light ahead, illuminated only by unending flashes of lightning, and making sure that every one of her limbs stepped one in front of the other.

Behind her was a gurgling roar and the scrape of claws against stone in pursuit of her. Hot breath moistened her ankles just as she threw herself onto the kitchen floor. Half standing, half on her knees, she slammed the door shut. The force of something ramming against the other side was enough to knock her back to the ground.

Mind locked purely on survival, cunning abandoned Jane as she scrambled to her feet and ran toward the first door she saw, leaving the threshold to Hell unlocked and unobstructed.

She pushed through the door as she heard the splintering of wood coming undone from its hinges and was met by a blustering downpour. Blinded by rain, and deafened by thunder, Jane continued to run despite the storm; from somewhere too close behind the beast howled.

She didn't get very far before her foot caught on stone and was catapulted forward until she splashed down in mud. Pain ricocheted from her ankle and seething a breath between her teeth only resulted in her inhaling a mouthful of slimy earth. Looming above her were two stone angels, one with outstretched wings while the other drooped over its grave. The cemetery. She turned to glare at the headstone that tripped her but was instead met with a bloodshot gaze and a flash of teeth as the beast tore into her leg.

Jane screamed as the saber-teeth sank deep into her calf and yanked her back through a slurry of mud and blood. Even as a delirium of pain washed over her, she grappled to hold onto the headstone nearest to her with a free hand, but her fingers slipped as the beast rattled her with a great shake of its head. Her blood foamed from its mouth and its growl pealed through her, just beneath the surface of her skin.

The world momentarily fell into a haze of oblivion as teeth grated across bone. Any semblance of time and place was lost beneath the blazing pain, even when the beast released her leg with a final shake of its jaws and pinned her beneath its broad body. She couldn't feel hardly anything below her knee. Would a limb even be attached there anymore if she dared to look?

Hot breath reeking of blood—Jane's blood—drowned her, even in her daze, as a claw pressed against her shoulder and pushed her deeper into the mud. Air rushed from her lungs and she couldn't breathe. The other claw caressed her face. Not to smother, but rather in an uncanny gesture that cupped her chin and canted her head to the side—offering it a perfect view of her throat. No longer was she its prey, but rather its plaything, she decided with a dread laced with red-hot pain.

The beast continued to idly toy with her face, lolling it limply from side to side as though she were nothing more than a ragdoll.

Rude to play with your food, Jane would have muttered if she weren't drowning beneath rainfall, mud, her own blood, and the beast's assertive presence.

All she could manage to think of was to beg for death, and to have such a death not be as horrid as being rendered a sloppish mound of blood and skin and clothing left to spoil in the cellar.

No.

She couldn't allow herself to meet that fate. She refused to die at the hands of a monster. Not yet, at least.

The beast pressed down onto her mouth, a claw tickling her nostril, when the dormant animalistic core of her brain suddenly took hold and she sank her teeth with a snarl into the taut, gray flesh. Rank blood flooded her mouth, then splattered all across the front of her as the beast howled and ripped itself away. She spat out the small bit of meat and a congealed residue remained on her tongue, bathing it in a taste and texture not too unlike mud.

A cold, piercing sensation resonated from her palm as the beast howled, and her fingers curled into an even tighter fist around the knife still held there. She screamed her own howl as she drew the knife upward and stabbed into the other paw that held her down. She pierced the beast's claw and forearm again and again until the whole limb, and her torso, were bathed in its rotted blood; she only dared to pause her assault when the skin seemed to sizzle beneath every puncture of her pin. The odor of singed flesh permeated through the rain.

A great weight heaved itself off of Jane, and she could suddenly breathe again. Desperately she inhaled gulps of air but paused to gag when she tasted the blood on her tongue and felt a sharp pain flare in her leg.

Through the rain, she could hear the beast whimpering as it mewled over wounds that steamed as it licked them.

Jane seized that moment to stagger back to her feet, grateful she still had both limbs—and run. Or at least run as fast as her ruined leg and slick mud would allow, toward the looming shadow of the Drowning House. She nearly wept with relief when her feet met wooden steps and the sturdiness of a front door. She had never been so grateful to feel wallpaper beneath her fingertips as she rushed inside and slammed the door shut behind her. Her fingers, glistening red, slipped and fumbled to lock the door just as the weight of the beast pummeled against the other side. Unlike the cellar door, the wood stayed.

Jane didn't wait another moment before stumbling further into the house, seeking sanctuary as another howl rang through the storm outside.

She did not know where she was in the house when she at last collapsed in a heap. Her fall was cushioned by ornate, plush rugs. Numerous Tiffany lamps illuminated by strikes of lightning bathed Jane in a multi-colored delirium as her blood seeped into the conservatory's rugs.

So much blood...

Through the pain humming across her body, she listened to the beast's assault on the front door, felt it through vibrations in the house's very foundations, until it gave way to silence, the drone of thunder, and Jane's dull heartbeat. She hoped that the beast retreated out of frustration and defeat like a pouting child so that it could continue mewling over its festering wounds, but she found her fingers curling into a feeble fist around the knife in preparation for another attack.

If the beast attacked again, Jane was unsure how well she could fend for herself as the periphery of her vision started to haze and she could no longer will her limbs to move. Beneath the floorboards, just as Jane was beginning to slip away, was a low, deep thump, like that of a heartbeat, resounding from the resting place of Old Man Hayes' book.

Jaaaane...

A horrible whisper, caressing her with a cold, unseen hand, was what coaxed her into a numb oblivion.

Blood.

So, so much blood...

Eleven

HEN SHE OPENED HER EYES, AN OVERABUNDANCE of flesh surrounded Jane, in columns and arches of red. It crafted the ceiling above her, the floor beneath her, the walls pressing against her in viscid swirls. What wasn't made of meat was pitch darkness that was hot and reeking and endless.

Rhythmic thrumming, almost like that of a heartbeat or a digesting intestine, jerked the fleshy mattress that pillowed her. To her right was a plinth of meat, and beside that was a fleshy stalagmite, giving the appearance of a lamp and chair.

She blanched as she looked around the chamber, noticing more furniture-shaped hunks of meat and bony protrusions that hinted at window sills, a door threshold, a fireplace, and shelves.

A heart. A gut. An organ. Jane was trapped in the vaults of some great organ, one that was some hellish mimicry of the

Drowning House. It was hot and damp and smelled foul, like being seated before a hound panting its rank breath into her face. The room—the *organ*—itself that was breathing.

How did she even end up here?

When she looked down at her leg, blood continued to gush from the wound in torrents that turned her skirt black. The skin there was ravaged in the jagged pattern of monstrous teeth that consumed nearly the entirety of her calf. Flaps of flesh hanging onto the wound by mere sinews wavered with the room's breathing. The ache she felt was but a distant echo despite her growing lightheadedness as memories of the beast, blood-drenched mud and cellars, and collapsing in the conservatory rushed back to her. She needed to run—where to, she'd decide on once she gained her bearings.

The flesh beneath her squished and she slipped on the slick viscera when she tried to stand. Blood and fluids splattered each time she fell. A sweet and coppery tang bathed her tongue, invaded her nose.

Paired with the pain in her leg, the organ-room refused to let her find purchase, and it seemed to wheeze out a laugh once she accepted that she was trapped.

She groaned, finding herself too exhausted to even attempt to comprehend how she came to occupy this nightmare-space, and halfheartedly gripped the pin-knife in her hand when she recalled she still held it. Her fist fell from her lap to be cradled by the flesh-floor and her nose wrinkled beneath the sudden smell of burning meat.

She wondered if the beast was here too. And if it was still hunting her. The thought made her breath snag as she paused to listen for *anything*. The slip of claws against organ-meat, the panting of angry breaths, the roars of a creature hellbent on vengeance. But there was nothing. At least not at first.

The first thing she heard was her name.

"*Jane...*" it was a sound that gurgled, the syllables bubbling from the back of a blocked throat.

She gasped and pressed herself deeper into the flesh-wall; her body was jerked by another undulating pulse.

If this chamber was meant to resemble the conservatory, then the walls tapered down into its doorway where the muted glow of two eyes peeked around a black corner. Then, crawling on its hands and knees, emerged what Jane could only describe as a demon.

She choked on a cry as the thing skittered toward her, closer and closer. It had claws that glinted with the same golden sheen as the many too-tight rings upon its crooked fingers and dug deep to grasp fistfuls of fleshy floor. Its wet breathing rattled between ribs that writhed within a smoldered chest.

Jane couldn't move, whether because of fear or pain or the inability to find a secure hold on the fleshy surface she was curled upon, she did not know. As desperately as she wanted to flee or hide, she failed to summon such strength into her limbs. She was held prisoner by terror. She shook, hair slick and plastered to her brows with sweat and blood.

The demon's body was covered with red, flayed muscle that bubbled with burns, boils, and decaying bits that hung on thin threads of flesh. Golden rings pierced its nipples and a rigid phallus, and from the piercings wept blood and gold. A fine, thick, burgundy-colored veil embroidered with golden tassels was draped over a head that was misshapen. Elongated in the shape of a muzzle, with the muted glimmer of sickly yellow eyes peering at her through the fabric.

A chill entered Jane's blood and a sizzling energy struck her bones.

It resembled the idol in the parlor room.

"*Jaaaaaane...*" The demon gurgled again, its voice androgynous but dreadful in its croaking intonation, and Jane wished for it to never utter her name, let alone speak, ever again.

Such a wish was denied as it groaned, quick and harsh, "*Jane!*"

Its breath filtered through its veil to disturb her hair; it reeked of carrion and sulfur.

Even when she tried to hold her breath, the sweetly bitter stench pried its way into her mouth, her nostrils, her very bloodstream.

A hand, red and raw, shimmering with a layer of pus as though freshly burned, raised slowly, and Jane held a breath as she prepared for it to grab her.

And she almost wished it had as it instead grasped the tasseled edge of its veil and pulled it back, taking with it pearly strings of raw fluids and strips of burnt infection.

Something *nearly* canine screamed at her, its flesh flayed off to reveal a living infestation of a face. Golden teeth ground against one another as gilded puss oozed from between them. More pus leaked from the slits of nostrils that ran the entire length of its snout to the ridged dome of its cranium, the sockets that loosely held bulging, asymmetrical eyes, and the piercings decorating bony arches of its cheeks and brows.

A tongue, long and serpentine, unfurled from its jaws as it gurgled out another, "*Jaaaaaaane!*" Gold bubbled in foam at the corners of its maw, from which dripped viscous saliva.

Slowly, the tongue inched toward Jane. Its movements were languid and winding, like those of a serpent—the very one that tempted Eve.

She at last found the nerve to scream.

With whatever strength remained in her limbs, she gave a yell and slashed the knife outward. As hot liquid spurted on her hand, the creature retracted with a piercing shriek.

When she opened her eyes, golden fluid stained her arm and

a wriggling nub of tongue sizzled between her feet. The stank of singed meat surrounded her as the floor in which her pin-knife touched, too, began to steam, smoldering like flame kissed by ice.

The demon screamed as it reared up on its knees, thrashing its head and sending gold to spatter across the meaty room.

"*JAAAAAANE*!" The demon's howls shook the organ-room as it clawed at its face, opening more wounds that cried gold. "*Jane, Jane, JANE—*"

Twelve

"JANE!" TERENCE'S BELLOW PIERCED INTO HER EMERGING consciousness as he gave her shoulders another shake.

Everything was a blur as the sounds of the world returned to Jane in ebbing waves. All she could discern was a muffled whimpering, but she came to eventually recognize someone—though there may have been several people all at once in a cacophony of syllables and weeping—calling her name. None of them were the demon, yet they all were. The floor beneath her was of wood, not flesh; the walls were periwinkle-blue and bookshelf-brown, not infection-red.

She couldn't register it fully until she felt the heat of a hand touching her, cupping her cheek, pressing against her forehead. She tried to open her eyes and was met with the bleary gray light of early morning.

She was still in the conservatory, and, despite the haze of her vision, she saw two figures huddled by the door. Mrs. Foster was watching with her hands clutched over her mouth as she tried to stifle the emotion that threatened to break its usual rigidness, and Ms. Hudson just gaped, the color otherwise flushed from her ruddy cheeks.

Terence was kneeling before Jane, his hair disheveled and face pale as he continued to touch her, patting her cheeks and shaking her shoulders in an attempt to rouse her. Again and again, he called her name, each time becoming clearer and less like the demon's gurgles as she was lured back into the world of the living. The stench of blood hung heavy in the air, metallic and bitter.

He muttered under his breath before he gathered her in his arms, sending a jolting ache up her left leg and a whimper from her lips.

Though the thought crossed her mind lazily, a string of terror weaved through her as she wondered where all the meat, all the blood, had come from, and why or how it ended up in Terence's cellar. Whose body had been down there? And how many?

Where had the beast gone? Why was everyone just standing here? Didn't they know they had to flee?

Jane whimpered again, unable to speak proper words.

As Terence carried her, she wanted to wriggle free. She feared that he was bringing her to the cellar to add her to those piles of meat, perhaps as punishment for her disobedience, and was to throw her straight into the beast's awaiting maw. Or maybe he was bringing her to lay before the idol, a totem of the flayed-faced demon in her nightmare, to butcher her for its amusement. Its gurgling cackle bubbled in her ears, burning hot with petty hate.

Her pulse raced through her as he brought her to the washroom, as he and the two women stripped her bare and dipped her into the steaming bath, as they mended her leg with thread.

Even as Terence set her in bed, she whimpered, speech slurred as she wailed about the beast, begging for him to let her leave and to keep the beast away.

All she could remember was seeing something vaguely resembling pain pinching his brow as the darkness swallowed her whole once more.

CHAPTER

Thirteen

THE PAIN IN JANE'S LEG AWOKE HER BEFORE SHE FELT the sting of daylight piercing through her eyelids. As she slowly came to, so did the looming shadow of a figure sitting at her bedside. She gasped as she rushed to prop herself up on shaking elbows, everything aching, but a hand came to her chest, gently easing her back down.

"Jane—stay..." Terence's rumbling whisper embraced her, timidly, as if she were an animal to startle or a doll to break. His face, partially obstructed by hair that had fallen loose, became more clear. He wore a dark robe, open to show the rumpled shirt and trousers underneath, and there was no sleep in his eyes. They had to them a pink dewiness that only came after one had a particularly wretched cry. He was quick to retract his hand, fingers flexing, as he returned to sit in the chair that had been pulled up alongside the bed. "Rest, please."

Jane continued to frantically blink the bleariness from her vision and the ache from her skull.

"Beast... a beast outside, the *cellar*—Terence," she blanched when she recalled those mounds of flesh, the slurping sounds as the beast lapped at puddles of some bodily goop. The stank of congealed blood still clogged her nostrils, the color of her stained dress was a residual crust against her flesh, the taste of blood in her mouth was an echo of last night's horror. She gagged. "W-We need to leave!"

I need to leave—I cannot stand to be here another minute.

A grim shadow inked across his features as he leaned forward and lightly cupped her chin between his fingertips with the gentlest pressure.

"And go where?" He whispered. "The roads are still flooded, we have no horse, and I reckon that you should keep weight off your leg for the time being."

Her heart was pounding, sending cold blood through her veins that muddied her mind.

We can go nowhere.

We're trapped—damned.

Those words felt too damning, as though they were the keys that locked her tightly shut in a cell where the beast would be in the corner, waiting to devour her. The demon would be crouched in an opposite corner while gurgling in amusement.

Panic was wracking its claws through her before settling in her throat to strangle her as she stared out the window, hoping to seek some hope for escape but instead saw the beast's snarling eyes, its snapping teeth, in the jaundiced aura of the still-clouded skies that wept more rain.

Jane swallowed down thick bile. No one would save them—save her. No one would tell her mother, her sisters, her father, what became of her until it would be too late...

There was the mumbling of someone speaking, but a touch on her cheek alerted her to Terence's presence still at her bedside.

"Jane," he murmured, gently. The gauze that wrapped around his hand chafed her chin as he drew away from her. His mouth moved as though he were still talking, but Jane couldn't hear him. She was too busy studying his wrapped hand as ice-cold nausea surged in her throat. For on the bandage was a mark, faint and pink as some wound beneath it started to bleed through. A wound that bled in the arched shape of teeth in the cradle between his thumb and pointer finger. She licked her lips, the phantom sensation of rotted meat weighing on her tongue.

Jane's teeth marks.

The taste of the beast's blood flooded her mouth, sour and like bile.

As she failed to retain a single thought that wasn't fueled by the pure animalistic fear to flee, she met Terence's eyes. A dreaded *knowing* made them go utterly dark.

With a sound caught between a choke and a hiss, Jane coiled back, clawing distance between herself and Terence, to get as far away from him as she could without falling onto the floor. Aches jolted up her leg with every movement.

Terence visibly withered, drawing into himself, as an expression of hurt flitted across his face. He leaned forward in his chair to stand with his arms extended at his side, palms up in a non-threatening display.

"Jane..." he started slowly, but it was no longer Terence that spoke to her. All she saw was the beast, dog-faced and blood-stained, standing in his place. She felt the scrape of its teeth against her bone; she saw the demon that wept gold, a monster that hungered for *her* blood.

But how?

How were man and beast one?

"No! St-stay back!" She snapped, holding out an arm.

Her heart lurched as he tried to come closer once more. "Jane, please, allow me a moment to—"

The words spat in her ears like the snarls of the beast, and instead of a mouth he spoke with a fanged maw, kind eyes became pinpricks of hellfire, and his hands curved into talons set on gutting her.

She screamed.

"*No*! Keep away—!" Jane fell from the bed, crashing to the floor in a tangle of ruined limbs and soiled sheets. Pain wracked itself all across her body and the sickly feverous delirium made her flesh clammy as she wobbled atop gangling limbs. She shoved past Terence and through the door, trying to ignore the screaming of her name as she ran away with a staggered gait. Her leg nearly gave out on the stairs, and she heard the demon's giggle rattle beneath the floorboards from its sitting room lair.

She ran until she was outside, drenched with mist-laden rain. She needed to run. She needed to escape. The Drowning House sought to drown her in her own blood, and she refused to meet her fate in the teeth of a beast who deceived her with the face of a friend.

She did not know where she was running to or where her intended destination was beyond simply being *away* from the Drowning House. Mud was caking her skirt, her legs. She felt it seeping into the bandage that swaddled her wound, seeping in to infect whatever the beast's spit hadn't already poisoned. Voices echoed in the fog around her, and with every tree or rising tombstone she passed she instead saw the flayed demon. And it was laughing with eyes that glowed gold.

Suddenly the earth gave way from beneath her as a foot tangled with her nightgown's trailing skirt. She slid through mud until she lost touch with the ground and was tumbling deep, deep, into what felt like an abyss. Something semi-solid, somewhat soft, and rank in smell, cushioned her fall, but not without knocking the wind out of her.

An eruption of ebony feathers and raucous caws swelled the air as ravens took to the skies.

Jane's body spasmed as she tried to gulp for air. And even then she didn't want to breathe. The sickly sweet scent of rotted, damp earth surrounded her. Crumbs of forest floor were sucked between her parted lips with every breath she took; grit cracked between teeth she ground against the rising pain.

The world buzzed around her, and she just wanted to sink further into the safety of the earth, wishing that perhaps this had all been a horrible dream and she'd wake up back in the safety of the hotel, in the bed beside her mother, who would be stained with and smell of her expensive watercolors. But the odor of something putrid reminded her that she was still in the marshes of Wolf's Run, and the stench was growing so horrid, accompanied by the discordant buzzing of flies, that it prompted her to at last open her eyes.

And when she did, she screamed.

The belly of Mistletoe's disemboweled corpse gaped at her, yawning and wide and spewing strings of grayed entrails. Spots of white writhed between the guts. Maggots, burrowing their way deeper into fleshy crevices reeking of old death. The mare's mouth hung open, showing the dried blood crusting her blunt teeth. Maggots wriggled among the folds of the savage wound that tore her throat, in the hollowed eye sockets.

Jane jolted upright but found herself slipping on the dirt beneath her, only it wasn't *dirt*. It was a pond of corpses. Some fresh, some old, some being only bones and teeth that stuck out from the pit of rot; antlers and hooves of deer, the jaws of foxes and dogs. With every movement, she sunk deeper into the bog of Hell.

The smell penetrated her very flesh, stuffing itself into her lungs so that she alternated between screaming and gagging, tasting death on her tongue. Her heartbeat quickened so fiercely it pained her, and it only grew worse as she felt the phantom sensation of maggots wriggling to make holes of decay in her already festering leg wound. A deer's corpse stared at her, its eye milky and gray and slowly being eaten away by a maggot in its very center.

Darkness suddenly fell over her eyes as someone grabbed her from behind.

"*Don't look*! Jane, close your eyes—*I beg you*—close your eyes—" Terence's breath was hot and ragged against her cheek as he hauled her free from the death-pit, keeping a hand affixed over her eyes. "Please, I'm sorry, Jane—oh God, forgive me—"

As he dragged her back toward the house, even when he scooped her into his arms to carry her, Jane struggled the whole way. She screamed and writhed. She tried to bite him, scratch him, but he did not release her. Her dread ignited into heart-pounding fear when they were back in the house. All she could think of was the cellar stained with blood, and that he was dragging her back to that hellish pit, to chain her to the walls with those discarded manacles and throw her directly into the beast's gullet.

Whatever the beast—*Terence*—wouldn't eat, then it would be thrown into the death-pit along with who knows how many other victims, how many other innocent girls that'd been lured to this drowning domain.

She was growling and snarling, becoming her own beast, as she flailed and grunted out, "Let me go!" again and again and again. Even when he set her down in the plush embrace of his armchair, the heat of the sitting room's fireplace stifling the air in her lungs, she continued to thrash.

When he at last stepped away, she pressed herself deep into

the chair to keep as far away from him as possible. Even when he offered her a blanket from the sofa, she curled further away from his touch with a hiss, and if the pain in her leg wasn't blazing she would've tried running again.

A swift sting of pride flared in her heart upon seeing a pained expression cross his features. He took a seat on the loveseat with the pathetic meekness of a dog tucking its tail between its legs. She would've allowed herself a smug smirk at the scene if her gut didn't skewer with nausea as an image of the death-pit flashed through her mind.

The two sat in silence as their eyes locked, Jane the rabbit arming itself with new teeth and Terence the wounded beast. Regardless of how real the beast was, and how possible it was that it and Terence were the same—if such even *was* possible—Jane's trust, security, and affection toward him faltered. And she was afraid.

He nodded to her leg. "Your wound will need to be cleaned again."

Jane followed his gaze to the soiled bandage, grime and blood staining in an elongated arch fashioned in the shape of the beast's maw. The rest of her nightdress was stained the brownish-gray color of the death-pit, and she couldn't help but once more imagine maggots finding their way into her dress, her hair, underneath her fingernails, between her teeth, in the back of her throat, between her breasts, into the depths of her festering wound. It was a notion that worsened her nausea and it must've been apparent because a hand braced against her chest, gently pushing her into the chair.

Terence must've left her at some point because he was suddenly kneeling before her with his arms full of fresh gauze, rags, and a decanter of water.

When he cupped her ankle in his hand, she started to jerk free of his grip but found the pain too unbearable to do so, and allowed her foot to settle into his palm. He unraveled the bandages, and Jane blanched at finally seeing the damage the beast wrought. It was jagged from the flaps of flesh that were mended back together by small, black stitches. Skin had turned red and purple by monstrous teeth as the wound wrapped around her calf. Dirt speckled the oozing wound, and Jane thought there was a maggot or two wriggling between the sutures.

Terence's hand trembled as his fingers hovered over the wound, the air hovering just above her skin. His touch was even gentler as he began to dab at the blood with a soaked cloth. He barked a sound Jane thought to be a sob.

"All of this... all of this is my fault..." he mumbled, wincing as tears glistened in his eyes. "This was never supposed to happen."

With little control over her mouth, Jane snarled, teeth bared with a harsh laugh, "Oh, really? I thought nighttime attacks of a wild beast were all a part of this house's charm."

That earned her a wounded glare from Terence as he continued dressing her leg. The bowl of water at his knee turned pink with clouds of blood.

"I shouldn't have ever let myself grow so fond of you," he said, which was enough to make something within Jane sting, even more than the alcohol he swabbed along her wound. His hold on her ankle suddenly tightened. "Now that that... that *thing* has tasted your blood, it will crave more. It is greedy in that way: more and more, a never-ending hunger for blood—*violence*—that which is not its own. It can never be sated."

"Well, what *is* that... thing..."

Terence sighed heavily, rubbing his face before running his hand viciously through his hairline. "It's a scourge upon my bloodline. It infects us men before lunging for the throats of those around us we love. It has infected me, my brothers, and our father.

All we've ever known is this infection, and my father and brothers have all fallen victim to it. And now you've become a victim, too," he said, with a lowered stare, dark, haunted. "I know not where or why this curse was birthed, all I know is how it isolated my family, and that bringing you here has been a mistake.

"All my life I... I thought..." his voice wavered, and he licked his lips in an attempt to tame his tears. "I thought I could be different from *them*. My father, my brothers—other men. I thought I could be a *good* man—a good *person*, Jane—and not some... some *monster* my blood, the title of manhood, demanded me to be—"

"Surely there's something you can do about it—to get rid of it." Jane only found herself speaking as a way to stop the keens of his anguish. Because it made something within her ache *for* him, and after falling victim to the teeth of his dark secret, she didn't care to do any sort of additional aching.

He shook his head. "Our father had once tried, in our youth. But our curse has kept us bound to this infernal marsh, and our resources limited. But, dammit, as brief as it was, we tried. Cheap spiritualists and self-proclaimed witches that sold useless tinctures and whispers of hope. After a time I felt more like an animal to be prodded at, even when I wore my human disguise, even when the sun was high—no longer could I tell when I was meant to be a boy or some hellish... *thing* to be examined and feared. Eventually, we were instructed to keep our heads down and to bear the pain as strong boys should, until I had grown too afraid to look up."

The hand that cradled her ankle shivered as Terence's resolve at last appeared to shatter. He slumped before her, shoulders shuddering as he started to cry. He bowed forward until his forehead pressed against her knees and he clutched fistfuls of her skirts.

"God—I beg for your forgiveness, Jane... This wasn't supposed to happen," he mewled into fabric stained with rot and blood.

"I—I tried to keep you as safe as I could, but I just... I couldn't help myself, I couldn't keep you away. This heart—this imprudent, *wretched* muscle—has damned you... and I will never forgive myself. My greed, my sin..."

The scene struck Jane as she let the heat from his tears warm her knee, the marrow of her bones, for what beast would weep at the feet of a lady wounded by his own teeth to plead her forgiveness?

A hushed whispering from behind her caught her attention and when she glanced over her shoulder, she caught both Mrs. Foster and Mr. Hudson huddled in the doorway. They watched them with a sort of relieved indifference that Jane was unsure how to feel about. Had they been witnesses to similar incidents? How many other girls have they seen damned to a similar fate? Jane, suddenly, hated them both. They knew about this beast, of blood that flowed beneath their feet. They knew and neglected to tell her the truth. She hoped that seeing her maimed was enough to tarnish their souls with guilt—that was if their souls weren't already immune to guilt. Her eyes pinched in a glare before she looked back down at Terence.

Unsure of whether he'd startle like a dog, quick to bite, she hesitantly reached out a hand and ran her fingers through his hair. He went still beneath her touch, not once moving to bite. His hair was soft, so unlike the mange of the beast. She couldn't help but stroke him as though petting a dog between its ears.

Bad boy, she thought with a forced scowl of indifference.

Perhaps she could've been more compassionate in her understanding of the apparent horrors he'd suffered since his youth, but she found herself lacking such compassion and in its place held a bitterness for the fact he'd nearly eaten her as a result of his negligence.

"Why didn't you just tell me?" She finally rasped out. "If I were trapped here, who could I tell? If you killed me, then your secret would die with me, and if I return to America, the secret shall be mine to keep out of gratitude and kindness."

He just looked at her warily, and she could feel the misery oozing off of him, completely and utterly palpable, with a taste like bad ocean air. Tears dampened his face, eyes red, and the sound he made to stifle his crying wasn't too unlike a mongrel's whimpering.

"I rather like thinking of you as a friend, but you test my trust, Terence," she said. He visibly flinched at that, a wounded crease between his brows, but he otherwise remained still as she swiped away a tear with her thumb. "If I'm going to have to spend another night here—and Christ knows how many more after—then I want to know how to survive."

Her hand then shifted down from where it stroked his hair to grip his chin.

Her newborn hatred stammered upon seeing his pink, tear-stained eyes. A broken man caging a broken beast just beneath the surface of his skin. But a beast was still a beast, and she refortified her resolve by digging her thumb into his jaw and tightening her face into something severe as she brought it close to his, so that they may share the same air. His cologne overpowered her with the scent of bergamot and lemon oil, but beneath it, she could smell the whispers of a mutt's fur and the cellar's gore-soaked damp.

"And you're going to help me. You understand this... this *thing* inside you better than me, than anyone in this house," her hold on him loosened—*Only because I pity the poor beast*, she had to remind herself, "You're the one that brought me into this mess, and I expect you to help me out of it."

Fourteen

A S A CHILD, MORE THAN ANYTHING ELSE, JANE WISHED to be Mary Anning. She wished she lived amongst those Dorset cliffsides, wandering the shores of the English Channel where she'd acquire fossils to sell; pieces of past animals, the imprints of their flesh, the remains of their scat, until she'd find her own new beast, just as Anning uncovered her *Ichthyosaur*—an utter accident.

Despite the purgatory of living in a day where such a desire from a woman was frowned upon while also not wholly discouraged, Jane sought to be a woman like Mary Anning. Jane wanted to discover monsters, and she wanted to be remembered for it.

So, Jane had become Mary. She referred to herself as such and often introduced herself as Mary, even to family who very well knew that she was born Janet Elizabeth Sterling; they would just smile and play along as such were the whims of imaginative little girls.

Mary was the girl who walked with her father in the woods and Great Lakes shores, collecting bones and discarded antlers and shells, and who was taught about the trilobites and mastodons that had once roamed in prehistoric Wisconsin. Mary wanted to be like her father and write books on her fossil findings. Mary wanted to be the one who presented lectures at the Smithsonian as she announced her own fossil discovery—a whole new prehistoric beast that would be as equally awesome and beloved as the newly discovered *Triceratops*.

However, after a while, once she observed how others would sooner flock to the musically-inclined endeavors of her sisters and mother—with their shared auburn-haired, red-lipped beauty that'd make the Pre-Raphaelite Brotherhood flush—than spare a moment to offer polite grimaces at her procurements of palm-fulls of *Brachiopods* or owl pellets with half of a mouse skull peeking out from digested fur, she concluded that Mary must leave. Envy was but a smoldering ember, then.

Putting away her father's textbooks to instead read *Scribner's Magazine* and *The Delineator*, Mary the Girl needed to be subdued and replaced by Jane the Lady if she were to vie for the attention her sisters received.

Mary had lay dormant since then, stifled and suffocated beneath layers upon layers of silk and lace and brand-new petticoats and decorated hats.

Jane never anticipated needing to revive that child within her to better understand a live monster that seemed intent on hunting her, and, somehow, resided within Terence like some parasite.

Just as she had done with the beast's pawprints, she attempted to rationalize it as though she were identifying a new fossil: to begin, she needed to excavate a subject from the earth; then scrape and clean away any unnecessary sediment to make the specimen more visible (quite important to have a gentle hand, to not scratch the precious find); next would be trying to compare it to other known specimens, though this was where Jane struggled as she didn't happen to know other beast-men or cursed folk that could provide aide or comparison. Where a fossil was found, the kind of rocks it was found in, would help in identification, according to her father, as sediments worked like a calendar, telling what era the animal died and further narrowing down its identity.

Terence's beast wasn't dead, and all that was here was fresh mud and reeds. The harder she tried to view Terence and the beast as specimens, the more her mind strained. It was pointless.

In the end, Jane's head only hurt. No longer could she imagine or ponder. She needed to dig, literally. She decided that to properly begin her understanding of the creature, she would need to begin by digging into earth—in this case, that damned cellar. It wasn't an ideal place to search, but it was at least a place to start.

As Terence finished cleaning the sutures on her leg, then her dress, she reached within herself, far and deep, to grasp the hand of Mary and pull her forward, inviting her help.

She tried to not frighten Mary away from the prospect that this task would not so much be an archeological dig but rather like taking part in some morbid fairy story, similar to the ones Emmy would read to her girls when tucking them in on chilly winter nights. Far too grim for little girls to read before sleeping, Jane thought, but she'd prefer them reading about *fictional* wolves gobbling up *fictional* girls.

"*Fetch* me my parasol, would you?" Jane said to Terence once he finished wrapping her leg. She did nothing to hide the emphasis she put on the word 'fetch.' She smirked at his visible flinch as he finished binding her leg. He kept his head low and his mouth shut as he rose, trudged to the foyer, and returned with her parasol in hand. He offered a hand to help her stand. She took it with a hum. "Such a good boy."

Without another word, Terence dismissed himself and disappeared into the hallway.

Like a dog to his house, Jane thought with a sniff. So much for him helping her. Then again, she wasn't too eager to be in his presence at the moment.

Using her parasol as a cane, she seethed as she rose from her seat. She cast a glance at the mantle and the demonic idol atop it, and she swore she heard the thing giggle. She offered it her middle finger before hobbling from its sitting room dominion.

In the kitchen, she looked to the damned cellar door and her heart thudded coldly in her chest. The door was closed, but it now sat crookedly in its frame. A padlock hung from its handle, and Jane wondered if one had always been there since she first set foot in the house but she just failed to notice.

"It usually works keeping them down there."

Jane yelped at the approach of a voice, jolting her attention away from the padlock. Mrs. Foster stood beside her, hands clasped before her, her mouth set in a grim line. Several pale hairs hung loose out of her bonnet. She wore a gray, exhausted pallor.

"How many have been kept down there?" Jane asked.

"At one time? Four," Mrs. Foster said too simply.

Three brothers, one father.

Four beasts in that basement, fur soaked with blood and teeth that gnashed with fury—four pairs of eyes that blazed with the fires of Hell.

"I think I would like to go back down there," Jane said, and it wasn't until she saw Mrs. Foster flinch in her periphery that she realized what she said. A hand flew to her mouth in a too-late attempt to capture the words.

"I-I... Miss Sterling, may I ask why?"

I need to dig.

"I want to learn about the beast," she said instead. She winced. "I need to at the very least *try*."

Mrs. Foster's nose wrinkled in a similar grimace as her eyes searched Jane's face. "Miss Sterling... I don't know—"

"May I at least *try*?" she repeated. *Unless you're willing to face your guilt in neglecting to tell me about what this thing was earlier and confess to me all you know.*

She held Mrs. Foster's gaze for a moment as the woman worked her bottom lip between her teeth. Jane held her chin up higher for a moment, and at last, the woman sighed, and she reached for her chatelaine. She didn't even need to rifle through the keys, her fingers instantly knowing which to retrieve as she opened the padlock.

She opened the door for Jane, who reeled back a step as she was slapped by the rank stench of rotten meat and mildew.

Jane gaped down into the abyss, the stairs leading down into darkness that the daylight of the kitchen dared not to touch. She stared intently, too terrified of seeing the glimmer of the beast's eyes amongst the glittering stones, and yet was too afraid to look away and risk the beast launching from the shadows to rip out her throat.

A warmth in her hand alerted her to the oil lamp Mrs. Foster lit and held toward her. She otherwise did nothing more to offer Jane assistance in her journey down below.

Neither of them said anything as Jane took the lamp and stepped back into Hell.

Other than the slither of fabric and the asymmetrical padding of her steps, all she could hear was the dripping of water on stone. The light from the kitchen was partially obscured by Mrs. Foster's silhouette in the doorway, but the lamp cast everything in a sallow-colored glow. The familiar bloody prints, the scratches in the stones—Jane paused to gag into her sleeve as the smell grew overwhelming. But she persevered until she reached the bottom-most step, being sure to sidestep the shattered remains of her lamp from the night before.

Beneath her bare feet was the crust of old blood and the muddy slickness of newer gore. A stray clammy glob of gelatinous flesh against her toes sent a dry heave flipping through her body; stomach still empty, she spat aside a shot of acrid, bile-tainted spit.

Once her gagging subsided, Jane continued deeper into the cellar. She made her way to the freshest pile of meat, half-eaten by the beast before she'd interrupted its meal the night before. Beside it were unused manacles, all open in anticipation to be latched on to whoever prepared them only to have run out of time to secure their locks.

With nausea threatening to overturn her guts, she turned away from the gore to instead look at the walls around her.

In almost every stone were symbols, etched in a script Jane found to be familiar. Crosses, unblinking eyes, six-petaled flowers, horse-shoes. In varying sizes and lengths and neatness, like the carvings beneath the guest room bed, Old Man Hayes' journal. Jane's fingertips tingled as she traced one of the crosses. She wondered if similar carvings could be found in every floorboard, windowpane, and brick within the house's very foundations.

Just how scarred is this house? How much of this ruination was from a madman's fear or a beast's wrath?

The more she looked around the higher points of the cellar, she saw places where crosses hung from the ceiling on frayed twine and thin chains. The army of crosses in the Wolf's Run marshes must've marched their way down here to hang their brethren.

To keep something out, or rather, and Jane found this to be the most probable, to keep something *in*. Bound to the cellar, the house, the land in which the Drowning House sat crookedly upon. But she doubted simple iconography harmed the beast. She was never a woman of faith, nor was anyone in her family. The only touch with religion any of them had was baptisms, communion, and weddings, but those were only out of obligation rather than faith. She held no fear nor reverence nor sanctuary in the symbol of the cross nor Old Man Hayes' wards. If she doubted the symbol, so would a beast and whatever companions it may have.

But while a cross may not do it harm, she thought back to when the beast attacked her, and the smell of its burning flesh as she stabbed it with her hairpin—her silver hairpin.

"Silver..." she hummed, in tune with the thrill of Mary's zeal thrumming in her chest, her blood. Silver, a holy metal—holy in its divine purity, to those who hold faith or superstition. Perhaps holy enough to harm something dark, evil—a beast from the marshes, or a demon from her nightmares—and that it was time for her to forgo sensibilities to seek the arcane for protection. She couldn't hold faith in religion, but she could possibly summon faith in purity.

As she lowered the lamp, there was a new glistening piece of meat in the pile of flesh beside her. It compelled her to look down— to a face that stared back at her.

She choked on a scream.

Among the bits of congealed meat, there was what looked like a shoddy theater mask. It had the rubbery outlines of a brow, nose, cheeks, an upper lip. Blood and threads of sinew coated it in an unsettling visceral pink, with gore bulging forth from hollow eyes, an absent mouth. Jane staggered back with a hand to her lips as she choked on a gag. No. Not a mask. A *face*.

Terence's discarded face.

She staggered back and rushed up the stairs as fast as she could, trying her best to not slip on the slick steps; she only slowed down as her leg groaned in protest. She was caught by Mrs. Foster. The woman steadied her before locking the door.

As Jane braced herself against the wall and caught her breath, she noticed that Ms. Hudson and Ruben had come to gather in the kitchen, and they watched her with a tired resignation in their eyes. She had an odd sense that she went through some rite of passage typical for staff of the Drowning House: venture into the darkened basement to gaze upon the ruined remains of the master cast aside when he turned into a beast, so that they may know his true nature.

"Well?" Ms. Hudson crossed her arms and raised a brow. "Enjoy playing in the blood?"

Jane glared at her. Beating the cook with her parasol was suddenly a very tempting thought. "Wouldn't be needing to play in blood if you would have just told me *that*—" she pointed to the cellar door, "—was what you were so afraid of on the first night!"

The cook bristled with a scowl on her mouth. "Wouldn't be so afraid if Mr. Hayes hadn't let his grief make him so lonesome that he'd call on us to make the house all special and warm just for your visit—"

"Georgianna!" Mrs. Foster's chatelaine jingled with her bark.

"You know it's true! And, besides, if he," Ms. Hudson now pointed to Ruben, who continued to wring his cap between white-knuckled hands, "would bite the bullet and take hold of a shotgun again, maybe then the poor thing would be put out of its mystery just like the last one!"

"Georgianna, that is *enough*!" The very cupboards rattled with the whiplike snap of Mrs. Foster's tone, even beneath the sharp silence that followed.

Jane had gone numb and swayed on her feet. What did Ms. Hudson mean? Had Jane truly been their executioner? Was it her fault that they were all summoned here—and subsequently trapped along with her—all in an effort to impress her and present to her a proper home, hiding the blood, flesh, bones, and horror that crafted its foundations and pulsated within its very walls? And was that why they'd neglected to inform her of the beast, in the hope that it'd eat her instead and leave the staff be for the time being?

Her roiling amalgamation of guilt and ire was nearly smothered by a morbid curiosity she mustered as she looked to Ruben. He was like a fresh colt, with his gangly limbs and knobby knees that shook as he shifted his weight from foot to foot. He avoided the gaze of everyone looking at him, chewing on his lip.

"What does she mean by 'the last one'?" Jane asked him with a snarl creaking between her words. She felt Ms. Hudson's scowl burn into her back.

His pale eyes darted between her, Mrs. Foster, and his cap. His throat bobbed as he worked down a swallow. "It was Matthew. Th-the one whom I..."

Ruben took another look around, and it was Mrs. Foster who spoke. "Matthew was 'the last one.' Ruben had been the one to..."

"Kill him." Ms. Hudson said with the bluntness of death.

Jane blanched. The recent murder of Matthew Hayes—it was committed by the young man standing before her, shivering like a pup in the rain? The bruises along his jaw suddenly resembled battle scars. Scars from a beast.

She couldn't help but laugh, a dry, husky sound.

"You? *You* murdered him? You... Why?" As soon as it left her mouth she knew the question was stupid. If he'd been attacked by a beast just as she was, he'd have every reason to murder the monster, regardless of whether it was Matthew or a beast.

Guilt turned Ruben's stare murky, his lips a stiff line. "Because he asked me to."

Suicide, then. Not murder.

"The body is buried in the yard," he continued, and Jane perked up.

A *beast's* body? That excitement returned to her chest, and she tried to focus on that feeling rather than the guilt that threatened to fester there.

"You hold that thought, and stay here," Jane hoisted her skirts and was prepared to move. "I would like to see this grave."

Before any of them could protest, she hobbled out of the kitchen and to the conservatory, every other step accented by the enthusiastic tap of her parasol against accursed floorboards.

The hairpin. She needed to find the hairpin and the last place she remembered seeing it was when she was lost in the delirium of blood loss in the conservatory.

As she entered the room, Terence jerked awake from where he slept in one of the plush armchairs. Blood stained the very fringes of its golden upholstery. He rapidly blinked the sleep from his eyes at her sudden arrival.

Jane didn't need to search for the pin for too long, as she found it on the sideboard. She strode over and took it, holding it up to twist it beneath the natural gray light filtering in through the skylight. Brownish blood still crusted the blade, and the ruby glow of the Tiffany lamps made those stains bleed.

"Jane?" Terence's bleary voice took her attention away from the hairpin. He slurred, "What is the matter?"

She arched a brow at him (though not for too long, as she still thought of the fleshy remains of his visage in the cellar). She turned to him and held out her hand.

"Paw," she said. A demand, one meant for a dog.

Without a word, he gave her his hand, placing it in the middle of her own, and she gripped it to stay its tremor as she used the pin to prick the heel of his palm.

"*Jane*?!" Terence yelped, more out of surprise than pain, but she didn't let him take his hand back. She watched as the bead of blood bloomed, without the steam of the beast's wound, nor the gold of the demon's.

She scowled as she licked her thumb and swiped it across the little wound, cleaning it.

"Roll your sleeve up for me, won't you?" She gestured to the arm of the hand she bit.

Terence furrowed his brow as he covered the arm, clearly skeptical. "For what reason, Jane?"

"I think I'm onto something," she said and held up the hairpin. "This is made from silver. When I stabbed the beast—er, rather you, I suppose—it was as though I burned it—" *Then I had a nightmare, and I saw... something, and it seemed adverse to silver as well,* "—I need to see if silver can protect me."

Terence searched her face, mouth tight. He nodded slowly. "Silver is the most pure of substances in many cultures," he mused aloud, almost to himself, as he began to roll up his shirt sleeve. "I suppose it'd be a protection for you..." He winced as he hissed, "Why hadn't I thought of that sooner?"

Jane didn't answer him and took him by the wrist. At first, she flinched as she came into contact with scar tissue at his wrist. The skin there was smooth, just like the scar she'd peeped across his throat, as if rubbed raw again and again, the skin burned away to never properly heal. As her thumb circled in the center of his wrist, Jane thought back to the shackles in the cellar. How long had he resorted himself to being chained and hidden, bearing such scars in an effort to protect others from himself? Her heart softened slightly. It all seemed so noble—maybe even good.

Terence's breath hitched beneath her ghostly touch; without a second thought, as she held it up, she kissed the pulse in his wrist.

A wordless apology—a silent recognition of his sacrifice.

She then looked further up his arm to the pockmarks of where she stabbed the beast. She leaned in close enough to feel the heat of his blood against her cheeks as she peered closer at the wounds, with their cauterized edges knotted like melted wax. She pricked the skin of his forearm just as she did with his hand, and swiped the blood away. The new wound wasn't at all like a burn mark like those scarring him now. It didn't sizzle, and she didn't smell burning meat.

Human flesh is unaffected...

Beneath her, she was acutely aware of the heat from his body flush against hers and the rise of his chest as another breath hitched. A blush crept up her neck to settle in her ears, and her silent vow to fear him further wavered.

Her eyes fell to his lips, shivering as they were parted with a low breath. She wondered if he enjoyed the sensation of her blood painting his mouth.

"Jane..." Terence started. His fingers curled until he caged her hand in a loose fist.

Jane's heart pummeled at her ribs.

Liar, beast, specimen. That was all he had become to her within the span of a single morning.

But he was a good specimen to her—

No.

Her heart couldn't be at war with her sensibilities like this. Not now, not when she was a prisoner in a beast's domain.

She suddenly felt a need to sink her teeth into him again, unsure of how else to channel the frothing emotions. But she stepped away before the urge germinated into temptation.

Without another word, she rushed from the room.

She had a beast's grave to desecrate. Such a task required no distractions.

Fifteen

RUBEN WAITED FOR JANE TO SHUCK ON HER BOOTS and a jacket before they walked out into the yard together. The storm had tamed itself to a gentle drizzle and mud sloshed beneath their boots as they crossed through the mist. The island was considerably smaller than the day before; Jane could no longer see the drowned carriage.

Near the kitchen's side door and within the cemetery, Jane noticed disturbances in the mud from the beast's attack. Even though it had rained, there were puddles of old blood in the slurry, and she looked away with a shuddering breath and continued following after Ruben as fast as her injury allowed. Wet mud and slippery organs felt too similar, she learned; in the mud around them were the beast's pawprints.

Like rows of teeth, the wood's trees rose through the mist

ahead of them.

Jane's steps faltered. Ravens lingered. They took turns swooping down to pluck choice bits from the corpses that flooded the death-pit there, and the ones that remained atop their perches offered her challenging stares.

"Must we go in there?" She squawked past a dry throat. She didn't want to be anywhere near the death-pit. She could still taste the decay and see those maggots consuming all that was once living.

Ruben paused to look back at her, but only briefly before continuing into the woods. "Lady Hayes said that the beast's bodies were to remain hidden and away from those of the family. We've been burying them away from the family plot."

Out of sight, out of mind.

Then how many of those graves do *hold a human body?*

Jane popped the collar of her coat so that the mink-fur lining could stifle the rising stank of rot as she followed in after him.

A rustling in the leaves drew her attention back to the wood's edge, though. There Terence lingered. He stood with his posture slouched, gaze shadowed by hair loosened by another chilled gust of November air. The edges of his overcoat flapped in the breeze and his hands hung at his sides as he watched her; a dog listless without an owner to guide his chain.

How long had he been following them?

Jane paused to rest against her parasol, puckered her lips in a whistle, and patted her thigh. "Come! Come, boy!"

There was a moment's hesitation before Terence crossed the threshold into the forest's realm of death-rot with stilted strides until he loomed beside her. Cast firmly downward to the leaves that clung to his muddy trousers and shoes, his hazel eyes were as dark as charred wood.

Jane forced a smile as she cupped his chin and gave it a scratch in a manner like she'd seen her sisters praise the hound Patroclus; fresh stubble chaffed her fingertips. She hated the sensation.

Nonetheless, she cooed, "Good boy!"

He gave no response to her, or her touch. His shoulders slouched further, his eyes dimmed until they closed entirely, and a new line formed between his brows as he breathed out a heavy sigh.

Jane's smile faltered. The novelty of teasing wore off if it garnered no response other than increased sorrow. Though her leg, the very one he'd nearly eaten, panged with every step and fueled new hatred for the beast, she failed to hate *him*. Not with how tamely he rested in her palm as her grip loosened and she traced lazy circles in the center of his chin with her thumb; she grazed his lower lip to part them just enough to glimpse his teeth, to ensure that they were blunt and human.

Perhaps she would've spoken to him, uttering a quick apology, if his eyes hadn't opened again and looked toward Ruben deeper in the woods.

"Allow me to help, Miss Sterling," Terence said and offered her an elbow.

Jane didn't take it and instead glared at him, as a jab of her own out of the shock of his formal addressing of her. He seemed to notice, furrowed his brow, and ushered her along with a gentle ghosting of his touch against the small of her back.

As they continued on, Jane also noticed how Terence held himself beside her, especially as the sweetly sickening stench of rot from the death-pit assaulted her senses. A wall for her to hide behind.

The ravens in the trees above cackled.

The beast wouldn't have been this gentle, Jane thought, as she felt another accidental brush of his touch against her back. She was certain it would throw her into the death-pit, not even offering her the dignity of eating her, leaving only scraps of a plaything for the birds to pluck at until even her bones were spent.

She took a moment to brave a glance at Terence, and saw his gaze fixated firmly ahead; his body blocked her view of the death pit, but she could still catch glimpses of rib bones, Mistletoe's bloated midsection. As he stepped on a branch, she thought it was the crunch of bone.

They reached the opposite edge of the wood, bordered by overwatered marshland rather than muddy lawn, and Ruben stood atop a ridge that overlooked another shallow ravine, much like the death-pit. Unlike the death-pit, shrubbery encased the ravine's bottom, with an 'entryway,' if Jane could even call it that, being a small tunnel formed by the brambles into a brown-shaded darkness.

Jane narrowed her eyes at Ruben, then Terence. "What's down there?" As if she didn't already have a guess.

"That's where..." Ruben hesitated, lips pursed, and glanced in Terence's direction.

"That is where we bury the monsters," Terence said at last, cold and grating, as he stared into the dim tunnel.

Jane hadn't noticed it before, but Ruben took hold of a shovel that lay just beside the tunnel's entrance and then made his way down into it, ducking his head to avoid the sweeping catch of the brambles.

She went to go in after him, leaving Terence to loom over the trail in a shadow of misery when he showed no sign of joining them.

The incline was slight, but enough to make Jane's leg ache as she followed in behind Ruben. With an offered hand he helped ease her down as the ground leveled into a small glade within the bramble bushes, wherein laid several mounds of dirt. Three of them, Jane counted, with one of them being considerably smaller than the rest, and the third dark with damp dirt. A fresh grave. None of them were marked.

Ruben stepped toward this third grave and, wordlessly, struck it with his shovel.

Jane watched as he began to uncover the body lying beneath, starting with the half-rotted shape of a wolf-like head, eyes bulging open and littered with the grit of dirt. Its lips were curled to show large, curved fangs the color of bone.

Once the abomination was unearthed, Jane was overcome with the desire to run. Curiosity held her firmly in place.

The body—or rather, *bodies*—lay curled on its side, and it was mangled. Warped and conjoined. There was the body of a beast, as wolfish and horrible as the one that attacked her, with moldy brown fur and flesh stretched over bunches of primal muscle, but from the torso burst forth a man. He undeniably shared blood with Terence. His sloping nose, heavy brows, and general visage of an utmost, tranquil melancholy reminded her almost *too* much of Terence, as he lay half-sloughed from the beast's body.

Matthew Hayes.

Blood turned the corpse's auburn-brown hair black, and bits of old meat clung to his beard. Two sets of hands melded together, twenty digits—ten of them blunt, ten of them tipped with claws— grasped at the dirt.

Matthew Hayes, wearing a beast upon his back as a coat.

A second skin.

Jane had been too enamored with the gruesome corpse to even notice the stench that permeated from it. She couldn't decide if it looked more like a man murdered whilst removing his (very ugly) fur coat or poorly rendered wax sculpture. But it was neither. It was a parasite broken free from the very parasite latched onto its back.

She gagged into her sleeve as she dared to step closer, brandishing the silver pin-knife. Her hands shook. She had never seen a human body before, let alone handle one post-mortem. But she summoned courage with a shallow breath. What was paleontology, and its adjacent sciences, but the desecration of antiquity and a disruption of its tomb?

Several bullet wounds marked the bodies of both man and beast, but the most savage one was the one purpling either side of Matthew's throat. The killing shot. Made by the man standing right beside her, resting against the shovel and with his face shadowed by his cap.

Three graves—two brothers and a father, Jane guessed.

Did Terence feel any semblance of loneliness, or dread, in knowing that they were buried, leaving him on his own? Did he fear which cemetery he'd be put six feet under if he, too, were murdered? Perhaps being trapped between the realms of brutality and dignity, not sure to which he belonged, was what was most lonely.

Wolves—and wolfish beasts, Jane supposed—were pack animals. They weren't manufactured to be without companionship. They required a pack. Jane had sensed that Terence had none, not now, or maybe ever.

Her heart pricked for him again, the fingers that cupped his chin itched, her maimed leg ached. Could a beast feel such loneliness? Was the beast more lonely, or the man?

She pushed these thoughts aside as she lowered herself into the grave, and brought the knife to the bullet wound in dead Matthew's throat. She punctured the skin, then slowly dragged it through the clammy gray flesh. It was like cutting through old leather, tough and straining, and no blood flowed, no fluid. Nor was there any steam or the smell of burning. She jerked her hand back with a gasp, deciding she'd never want to feel the sensation of gliding a blade through a human corpse ever again.

Jane then did the same with a wound on the beast's chest, and the skin was barely cut before she heard telltale sizzling. There was only a whisper of steam that rose, but the skin bubbled and blistered and festered as she continued to drag her knife through. And it was unlike cutting flesh, not like when she pierced Matthew's hide. The blade made its cut as swiftly as cutting melted butter.

When Jane brought the blade back, brown rotted fluid continued to boil along its length. To test her theory once more, and perhaps out of impulse as she was tired of the thing staring at her, she pressed the knife to the beast's dead eye until it burst with an audible, squelching *pop*. Steam fizzled from the oozing socket.

Morbid triumph flared in her chest.

Silver could be her salvation against the beast, should it decide to attack again. She was still far from properly understanding it—if anything, it'd only made the creature more confusing as she wondered how similar their behaviors may have been to wolves, why they had been adverse to silver, and what it was about their physiology that allowed a man to share a body with them—but it was still *something*. It was a start, and it was a semblance of protection.

Excitedly, Jane began to clamber out of the grave when she slipped upon the muddy ground that surrounded Matthew's body. Only it wasn't mud, but rather more of the beast's hellish skin that seared beneath her hairpin's silver touch.

Ruben caught her before she fell and steadied her.

When she looked up to thank him, she was met with him staring into the grave with wide eyes and a slack jaw. The grip he had on her arm shivered.

"Something the matter?" She asked, as if she hadn't just desecrated a wolf-beast's grave.

It was a long couple of moments before Ruben spoke again, his throat bobbing with a forceful swallow. "He wasn't like that when I buried him."

CHAPTER

Sixteen

TERENCE, AS STILL AND RIGID AS A CHIPPED GARGOYLE, was waiting for the pair when they emerged from the hidden cemetery, and the three of them returned to the house in silence, tension hanging too thickly between them to be broken.

Afternoon was already bleeding into early evening, and after a bath and a supper of vegetable soup, Terence asked if he could help Jane to bed.

With the pin-knife clutched in her palm, she let him.

As he carried her to bed, a hand braced between her shoulders and the other beneath her knees, confliction returned to Jane, once more accompanied with guilt. The tenderness in which he handled her as he set her down in bed, as though she were a china doll that'd shatter beneath a poorly placed breath, and tucked her beneath layers of fresh, lavender-scented duvets and quilts, betrayed the brutality of the beast.

The beast wouldn't have done that *for* her. The beast wouldn't have locked the door behind it to protect her from itself; surprising herself, she was sad to see Terence go, and nearly begged him to stay by her side.

Jane sunk further into the old mattress and she snuggled deeper into the protection of Terence's nest of blankets, but she couldn't bring herself to fall asleep despite her exhaustion. The ache in her leg was felt throughout her body, reminiscent of monthly cramps, and an itching fear persisted in her brain as she watched the light of day fade into the darkness of evening. Toying with her silver pin-knife did little to ease the anxiety. It worsened as familiar screams wormed their way through the Drowning House's pipes. Screams that morphed into growls that were utterly nonhuman.

Jane tried to seek security in her blankets, anxious that the beast could smell, hear, *taste* her from its prison in the meat-stained cellar. Her unease, the pain in her leg, throbbed fiercely as she heard the echo of wood splintering from somewhere downstairs, the thundering of something dragging itself up steps, and the gallop of something coming down the hall, accompanied by the clinking of metal against wooden planks. Her heart was in her throat at the familiar rhythm of claws scratching at her door. She gripped her knife, prepared.

Then the room shuddered and bowed as something smashed against the door.

Jane didn't know whether it would be best to hide or prepare to run, but all she did was remain frozen right as she was and tightened her fist around the knife—and hoped for some kind of protection in Old Man Hayes' wards.

It only took one more crash against the door for it to break down, sending oaken splinters flying into the air to shower Jane in bed. The beast shook itself in the doorway, manacles and chains hanging broken from its throat and wrists.

Jane's blood ran cold at the sight.

Christ—It broke free to get to me—

The beast snarled and trained its yellow eyes on her, baring teeth that were slick with the fluids of hunger.

Just as it lunged for the bed, Jane rolled onto the floor and, as swiftly as her body would allow, she scrambled to her feet and out into the hall while the beast tangled itself in her mass of blankets and pillows.

All that occupied Jane's mind was finding a place to hide. But if the beast could break free of chains, then where else was there in this infernal marshland she *could* hide?

Her nerves steeled themselves upon realizing the need to fight back, but when she clenched her fists, she noticed the absence of silver in her palm. Looking down, both hands were empty, and she swore. She must've dropped the knife in her escape.

She was struck with a cold arrow of hopelessness that damp-ened her pace. Unless she could find a weapon, especially one of silver, and somehow find a way to hide from the seemingly invincible strength of the beast, then she would have to accept the fact that she was to be another corpse to add to this marsh's landscape of death, mangled or shot—

Shot.

Suddenly Jane saw an image of a gun—a hunting rifle. The Win-chester in the sitting room. The bullets displayed along with it likely weren't silver, but what creature would survive a shot to its muzzle?

With as fast of a pace as she could muster, Jane continued her mad stagger down the hall, stumbled and partially fell down the stairs, and hurried into the sitting room where the Winchester rifle was waiting for her on its perch over the mantle. With a hiss, she smacked the idol aside to silence its snickering and a shock jolted through her hand. Upon hitting the statue, the beast screamed upstairs.

Jane grabbed the gun, its slim body fitting comfortably beneath her palms, and she snatched the bullets displayed underneath it. Her fingers fumbled to load it to the beat of claws pounding down the stairs. The beast's maw was agape with a slobbering snarl as it rounded into the sitting room; dangling chains jangled, but dried blood muted the sound.

Amidst her panic, she dropped all but the one bullet that she managed to load into the barrel, and she barely had time to cock and fire it just as the beast pounced across the threshold.

The room was illuminated with a blinding flash and the whole house reverberated beneath the resounding shot. The power of the rifle kicked back into Jane's shoulder with a crack, sending her flailing into the fireplace. She winced, both at the sharp pain in her chest and in anticipation of the beast's teeth in her flesh once more.

But she must have hit her mark because she didn't feel the beast upon her. The thing reeled back with a fierce whine as blood spilled from the juncture of its shoulder blade and thick neck.

Blood splattered the walls, the flowering horn of the phonograph, as the beast shook its head with a gurgling scream. Even more of the muddy blood stained the guts of the house as it turned and ran, finding its escape into the night through the kitchen side door.

†††·†·†·†††·†·†·††·†·†·†††

No sleep was had the rest of the night.

Even if she wanted to or tried, Jane didn't know if she *could* sleep. Every time she closed her eyes, all she saw was snapping teeth stained with her blood, the sound of hungering to taste her once again, the laughter of the burnt-faced demon that wept gold, the odor of its organ-room and the death-pit.

She remained in the sitting room, stationed before the windows she propped opened despite the rain, with the Winchester aimed toward the darkness as every one of her senses strained to catch any sign of the beast's presence. She didn't dare to move to retrieve her knife.

It wasn't long after the beast escaped into the night that Mrs. Foster came careening down the stairs, her silver hair bound in a loose braid and a shawl across her shoulders. Without her uniform or her chatelaine, she appeared so frail, and the fear that aged her as she gaped at the blood and broken wood littering the house turned her pallor sickly. A hand was pressed against her open mouth when she looked at Jane.

Jane refused to lower the rifle as she offered a sideways glower.

"How long have you known about this thing?" She asked, curling her lip into a sneer as she turned to look back outside.

Mrs. Foster was silent for a long time as she watched Jane before at last retreating with quiet steps.

Jane expected her to have gone back to bed, returning to her quiet ignorance and turning her head to look the other way from the beast's destruction. But then she returned to the sitting room with two cups of tea, setting one on the desk beside Jane. The desk no longer held the fossils, most of them lying on the floor in broken pieces of stone and ancient bone.

Mrs. Foster sighed as she took a seat in Terence's armchair. She nudged aside a large splinter of wood with the toe of her slipper.

"I'm very sorry that you have been... dragged into this hell, Miss Sterling. My family has been employed by the Hayes since the days of Terence's grandfather, as have Georgianna's and Ruben's families. Secrecy was something bred into our very blood. Not even my husband knew the true extent of my duties here. But even then, rumors of the Wolf's Run Beast have always been associated with the Hayes name, as villagers like to rumor that Grandfather Hayes made a deal with the Devil for wealth and a nice little house on the hill that'd be impervious to the marsh's flooding."

Deals with the Devil... Jane's eyes flickered to the idol that watched the two women from where she knocked it to the floor. *How many of Old Man Hayes' wards were truly wards or signatures of hellish agreements?*

Her attention was brought back to Mrs. Foster when she took hold of the end of one of her gown's oversized sleeves and peeled it back to show the rest of her hand.

Jane winced at what she saw.

The woman's hands, wrists, and forearms were riddled with scars. Small, and arched, in the shape of hungering, fanged mouths, others the long rake of beastly pups' claws. It gnarled the skin, and the pinky finger of her right hand was missing entirely.

"I had a hand in raising the boys. Terence was most often my charge," Mrs. Foster continued as she ran a thumb over the nub of her missing pinky. "Every night I would witness the sweet boy I helped dress in the morning become a monster as the sun dipped beneath the horizon, and not once had I ever had an explanation for it. It just... was. It was their nature, and all we ever knew was that it was a secret we were never to speak outside the house or to anybody that wasn't ourselves or our employers."

Covering her hands, Mrs. Foster closed her eyes as she took a sip from her tea, and Jane was almost offended at how calmly she spoke about the beast that'd nearly killed her on several occasions, and left its mark on a young Mrs. Foster.

At the same time, she imagined Terence as a boy, as gentle and kind and wide-eyed as he was as a grown man, if not more so. Then she thought of that child being torn apart each night, replaced by an abomination hellbent on tearing flesh asunder, and swallowed down the lump forming in her throat. The ache in her leg stuttered her growing sympathy.

"How can you speak so... sweetly about that thing?" Jane muttered, words wavering.

"Because I pity it, Miss Sterling. I pity *him*," Mrs. Foster nodded to the windows. A distant howl rang out across the night. "He's tried to be different from them, his father, brothers, grandfather. They weren't bad men, but they were... *men*," she said with a grimace of indifference. "Their afflictions let them give into their isolation and the coldness and lovelessness that tends to accompany manhood. Love, in every sense of the word, was a thing they dejected."

Jane found herself thinking back to the visit to the university gardens in Cambridge, how Terence allowed her to ramble without ever interrupting her with his own thoughts on the matter until she was finished and seemed attracted to her company, the kindness he had shown to both her and her mother by what must have been a natural goodwill that'd resided in his spirit. He'd shown himself as a man with the capacity to love, seemed so desperately eager *to* love, and yet the beastliness of his bloodline—the beastliness of their day's expectations of his sex—kept him restrained.

"I think I pity him, too," she said, her hold on the Winchester losing its security.

After finishing the rest of her tea, Mrs. Foster sighed. "Well, best of luck to you with this hunt, Miss Sterling. I think I shall return to bed for a little while more before trying to clean this mess."

Mrs. Foster left both her and Jane's cups when she left the room, and Jane didn't release a breath until the sound of footsteps faded up the stairs and she heard the shut of a bedroom door.

✝ ✝✝ ✝ ✝ ✝✝ ✝ ✝ ✝ ✝ ✝ ✝✝ ✝

THE GRIM, PINK-HUED GRAYNESS OF DAWN LEAKED ACROSS the yard, turning the fog into a silvery mist that both hurt and soothed Jane's eyes if she stared into its depths for too long.

From upstairs she heard movement as the rest of the house roused for the day, and she wondered if Ms. Hudson and Ruben heard the upheaval of last night.

Jane scoffed. How could they not have heard a rifle firing in their house? And why did neither of them even bother to see if she was alive or if she needed any help? She tried not to hold too much anger, for she didn't know if she would be so chivalrous herself in a similar situation. She, too, would wish to hide rather than risk the beast turning on her.

There was a groan that echoed from deep within the mist that jolted Jane back awake and her grip on the rifle suddenly tightened, prepared to fire at any shape that even vaguely resembled that of the beast. Her heart was thrumming and her tongue swiped across her chapped lips as she awaited for the thing to emerge.

A silhouette did come into view, but it was staggering and wheezing. The beast seemed completely disinterested in its previous hunt from the evening as blood leaked thickly like mud from its mouth. Its throat was still stained red and Jane wondered if it were just now suffering the effects of the wound and at last breathing its final breaths.

She only grew more confident in her suspicions as the thing began to mindlessly pace in the yard mere yards away from the front door. She wrinkled her nose as the distant, rosy hue of dawn began to wash across its form.

It was truly an ugly animal. Something bent and broken that ought to be dead. The longer she stared at it, the more it started to adopt the shape of a prehistoric beast she could at last understand, even if only a little. A *gorgonopsid*, perhaps, or some other creature that was too much of a reptile to be classed a proper mammal and too much of a mammal to be classed a proper reptile. The thing doggedly pacing the yard had her imagining those beasts caught between identities and worlds.

She thought of Terence and the beast held within him. It was everything he couldn't let himself become: ravenous, violent, wrathful, soaked in blood, simmering with frustration of barely contained grief and being unable to secure his own identity in the world, just as Jane had been when vanquishing Mary in her youth. He was a powder keg that burst every night as the sun set, only to have the cycle repeat again, and again, and again, never once finding peace or healing, for men were expected to bear their wounds and carry on.

With a huff, Jane lowered the rifle.

At last, the beast raised its head in a wounded, piercing whine that made Jane clamp her hands over her ears. A pealing, hollow shriek of the dying. A sound seeking some savior or some other companion to join it in death—only to be met by silence as plumes of mist feathered from jaws stained with carrion. Traitorous pity stitched at Jane's heart.

As the howl rattled to its end, the beast collapsed to the ground, its sides deflating upon uttering a final wheeze.

Jane didn't know how or what she was meant to feel upon the sudden defeat of the beast. But she did know that she didn't feel victorious, only ashamed, especially as the corpse continued to twitch.

Her gut ran cold. She needed to go out there and finish this deed, either to properly earn a sense of victory or to put the creature out of its misery.

She kept a free hand braced against the wall as she hobbled to put on her coat and, using the Winchester as a cane every other step, went outside.

Mist cloaked her and she raised the rifle as she approached the wheezing beast. Blood continued to pool from its gaping mouth, and it whimpered in a way that made Jane falter in her steps. It whined with the pain of a wounded hound.

Jane held her breath and tried to will herself to raise the rifle to shoot. But a thought stayed her hand. If she planted a bullet in the beast's skull, would she also kill Terence along with it, just as Ruben did to Matthew? The two were linked to one another, whether it be physically or spiritually, and if she could bite its paw and leave a wound on his hand, she could only assume a shot to the head would end them both. The sin of ending a human life was a mark her soul lacked the courage to bear. The rifle started to shake in her hands as one of the beast's eyes rolled to meet her gaze.

There was no more time to consider the topic any further when the beast's body jerked, and in her fright, Jane failed to raise the rifle to deliver a killing shot. She just yelped and backed away from the convulsing corpse.

The beast's paws began clawing at the ground, flexing and grabbing at the grass in an action too much like one that'd belong to human fingers with human joints. It was as if it were trying to grab fistfuls of grass in an attempt to drag itself through the dirt, across the yard, and toward the house—toward Jane. Then the skin began to peel.

Discarded pieces of hairy flesh were scrubbed away by the grass, the claws fell away like rotted teeth, until two human hands remained, sticking crudely from the beast's body.

Something in its torso, between its ribs, began to writhe. Not in the rhythmic way of breathing, but rather from something wriggling around within a costume, a parasite wrestling for dominance.

Jane gagged but didn't dare to touch the body, as those *human* hands continued to pull themselves forward, ridding themselves further of the beastly pelt. In a burst of blood, they at last hauled a body from the beast's now hollowed torso. The corpse deflated as the man continued to pull himself free. There was the sound of rib bones collapsing upon no longer possessing a thing to cage.

It was eerily similar to the image of the man-beast abomination buried deep in Matthew's grave.

Terence groaned after pulling his legs out from the beast and curled into a fetal position, allowing the rain to wash away the discolored blood painted across his naked body.

Despite everything in her body demanding that she stay put and return to the house, Jane dropped the Winchester and hurried to Terence's side. She knelt beside him and tried to not be bothered by the fact he was utterly naked and had clumps of gore caught in his hair.

"Terence," Jane didn't know what else to say as her hand hovered over his shoulder, and she winced seeing the mark where her shot clipped him. The wound continued to weep blood, oozing.

Would a bullet need to be fished out? Or I can just let it scar over—that would be far easier...

It would serve as a reminder for the beast.

He groaned as he rolled onto his side, burrowing his face into the grass. Chains clinked around his wrists, his throat, the flesh beneath them rubbed raw and bleeding.

Jane sighed, shucked off her coat, and draped it across him. She nudged him with her foot. "Come on, boy—*up*. Let's get you washed."

Beside them, the beast's pelt began to audibly sizzle, melting down into an acidic sludge until the marsh's mud soaked the evil back into its accursed depths.

† †† ‖ † † ‖ † † ‖ † † ‖ † ††

TERENCE KEPT SILENT AND HIS GAZE CAST DOWN AS JANE guided him to the washroom upstairs.

She threw her coat, now soaked and crusted with the blood, to the corner, ran water until the room began to fog with steam, and eased him into the tub.

At some point, Mrs. Foster rushed in, as poised as ever, and unlocked the manacles clinging too tightly around his throat and wrists. The skin was blistered and bled the moment it was exposed to air.

With the soap and cloth she found in the cabinet, Jane began to slowly swab away blood until the water clouded a murky maroon color.

Her scrubbing paused, though only briefly, as she washed his back. A latticework of scars stared at her. A cross-hatching of pale welts and fissures left in the wake of claws, the arched imprints of beastly teeth. A map of a lifetime of horror.

And I've added yet another mark.

A forefinger traced over a particularly brutal scar that slashed down the length of his shoulder. She bit her lip as she wondered how Terence had gotten such scars, how young or old he had been, and which skin he was wearing when he got them—beast or man. His skin jumped beneath her touch, but he otherwise remained deathly still.

Jane sighed and replaced her fingers with the cloth. "I'm sorry I shot you," she murmured.

He gave no response. He only stared ahead with a numb gaze.

"This blood isn't mine," she tried again. "It's yours."

A flush rose in her cheeks as she'd grown increasingly aware of the naked man beneath her hands. She shivered. She needed to remind herself she was washing a dirty dog—and a bad one, at that—not a human man.

Terence grumbled and winced as she lightly dabbed around the bullet wound.

"I'm sorry," she repeated in a hushed murmur and pressed the rag over the shallow hole. "I needed to do something to save myself. You ought to count yourself lucky that I am a horrible shot." She laughed at her joke, mostly for her own sake, but the laughter softened into stiff silence again once she realized Terence wasn't laughing with her. His gaze was still firmly fixated on the opposing wall, his mouth set in a thin line.

"This was how my brothers died," he mumbled instead. He raised a hand from the water to cover hers that'd been tending to him. "They killed themselves, one by ingesting lye as a boy and the other asking to be shot in the night—hunted like an animal."

Jane went still, unsure of how else to respond to him. She thought of Matthew's grave, of the bullet wound that marked both man and beast, not too dissimilar to Terence's own wound.

"I refuse to die like an animal," Terence said firmly, his grip tightening over hers. "If I die by *its* hand—*because* of it... then that means it has consumed me, and that it has won. And I refuse to let it hold that sort of sway over me."

Jane worried her lip between her teeth as she traced her gaze over the scars all across his back. His skin was etched with his efforts. Hidden beneath pressed clothes, high collars, perfumes, and charms. In her hands, she held a gentleman in wolf's clothing. She was on the cusp of understanding it—wholly.

His hand abandoned hers to cup his brow. His shoulders slumped and a thin whine pealed from between his lips. "It's hopeless."

"For now," Jane whispered, daring to reach and tuck loose hair away from his face. The touch was featherlight and hesitant. She placed the cloth on the edge of the tub and rose to her feet. "In the meantime, I'm sure cleaning yourself and getting some rest isn't too hopeless a task."

She left Terence to soak in the tub, closing the door behind her. It wasn't until she was on the other side that she realized how steeped in blood and misery's coppery scent the washroom's steam was.

She lingered at the door, though, her hand cradling the knob as she rested her forehead against the wood with a low sigh. Rain pounded against the roof and she hissed a seething, "*fuck*" into the air before her. Hopeless, all of it hopeless, just as Terence said. The marshes were hellbent on killing her, it seemed, and she doubted that she'd ever make it back to Cambridge, if not in one piece.

"Thank you, Miss Sterling," Jane jumped and saw Mrs. Foster standing beside her, still holding the chains. She sighed as, with a free hand, she returned a stray hair beneath her bonnet. She then laughed, a mirthless, breathy sound, as she shook the chains. "You know, the blacksmith in town used to be on the Hayes' salary."

The dry laugh and jangling of chains continued as Mrs. Foster turned to walk down the stairs, leaving Jane alone in the hall.

Jane couldn't place if it was the exhaustion in her bones, the pain she felt everywhere, the irritation of wearing stale, under-styled dresses continuously stained with blood, or just a growing desire to give up and let her body be claimed by the marshes, but she somehow mustered the strength to limp back to her room. The echo of bloody chains chafing followed after her.

† †† ·† † ·†† † ·†† †† · †† †

JANE LEFT THE GUEST ROOM FOR TEA AND ENRICHMENT sometime around the noon hour, but she paused before she even descended the first step of the main stair. In the entryway Terence and Mrs. Foster were crouched together on the floor, sweeping up wooden bits and stains of the beast's muddy blood.

His sleeves were rolled up to reveal arms corded with muscle and marred by even more of those pale scars as he continued picking up splinters of wood he cradled in a large palm.

Like a fossil with battle scars, waiting to be deciphered.

Their silence was heavy and tense; Jane sensed that this wasn't the first time Terence needed to assist in cleaning up a mess, though it was the first time in a long while.

Deciding she could go without tea, she quietly turned on the stairs and returned to her room.

Seventeen

ANE COULDN'T QUITE PLACE WHEN MUSIC BEGAN TO flitter through the house, but at some point, the distant pluck of the harpsichord drew her attention from redressing her leg in the washroom.

For most of the day, she had been alternating between states of fevered wakefulness and restless dreaming, keeping to the guest room and away from the staff, Terence, and any signs of the beast. However, the beast still seemed intent on seeking her out despite the daytime hour. For she dreamt of it, but also not. For it was also Terence, wearing the face of a beast, with yellow teeth and yellow eyes flashing down at her, dark hair bristling across a naked, scarred body, and claws curled in their eagerness to claim her. And he did claim her—biting her, drinking her blood, marking her as his own, as she writhed beneath the Terence-beast with a whimpering moan.

To be afraid of him or to desire him, to crave for him and his salvation, she couldn't decide. For the eroticism this nightmare held her with was tender, but the suckling of his fangs was a white-hot pang—an affection battling with the monstrosity lurking just beneath the surface of his skin. Skin that sloughed off to plop beside her on the mattress with every thrust of his body, revealing more of the beastly fur underneath, little by little.

He ravished her. That was when she had woken up with a start. Sweat clammed her skin, pressing her dress flush to her heated body, silhouetting peaked nipples and heaving breasts. Her throat was raw and every attempt at swallowing was like gulping down sandpaper. The Terence-beast's touch was still imprinted on her thighs and hips, branded into her skin in a way that itched with a burning shame.

That was when she heard the music. It was calling to her, pulling her to its composer with a blood-red string that wove between her ribs.

As she listened to the distant din of the harpsichord, she wondered what emotion inspired its composition this time. Its sadness made for an alluring tune. Perhaps that was why such music had been so attractive in the first place: the knowledge that a man caging such violent horror just beneath his skin was capable of forging beauty and kindness beneath gentle fingertips.

With this attraction had festered guilt, manifested in the Terence-beast that'd pinned Jane to her bed in her fever dream. The two emotions took hold of her hands to coax her to the stairwell.

She made her way downstairs and kept her footsteps as light as possible so as to not disrupt the music, especially when she peeked into the sitting room.

Terence sat slouched at the harpsichord. The notes he played were slow, his fingers listlessly plucking at keys with no intended rhythm. He didn't look any better than when Jane last saw him. Hair hung limply in his gray face, which was shadowed and drawn with deep lines that considerably aged him; silvery stubble roughened his chin. His whole figure sagged with an ashamed, lonesome melancholy that urged her to make her presence known by resting her hands atop the instrument.

She frowned when that failed to get his attention, so she lightly plucked at the keys closest to her, inspiring an uneven melody, and knelt before him with her fingers laced atop his knee so she could cradle her chin between her knuckles.

"What's eating at you?" She asked, tilting her head and grinning, aware of her words' double meaning. "What emotion is inspiring you this time, maestro?"

Sorrow, I hope. Perhaps even a twinge of guilt.

Again, Terence didn't acknowledge her. Instead, he continued to pluck away at the instrument's keys. "You should leave. Run away while you still can."

Jane couldn't help but scoff out a barking laugh, she couldn't help it. "If I could run away I would've done so already. Do you think I'd intended to have 'becoming dog food' on my itinerary when I left Milwaukee?"

A heavy breath rushed from his nose. His eyes failed to focus.

"My brother Elias killed our sister, mauling her by accident, then himself with poison," he whispered. "Matthew never took a wife nor any friendly companions for fear of what he'd do to them. Our father made our mother weary and die at an early age; her heart simply gave up. And we could never grieve—Father wouldn't allow it. To grieve was to be weak... I couldn't imagine doing worse to you, Jane."

"Damage has been done, I'm afraid," Jane shrugged and tensed her fingers.

"All of this is my fault…"

It is.

She squeezed his knee. "Well, you have no control over the weather nor do you have control over the waters of the marshes."

"But what about myself?" He shook his head, sneering as his lip trembled. "I thought I had control. I thought I knew what I could do to keep others safe from me so that I would not just become another shallow mound of earth. I—I shouldn't have let you come here."

She squeezed his knee again. "And yet here I am, and you certainly aren't going to magically resolve everything by moping about it."

He said nothing, but tears caught in the fissures of his face as a sob heaved from his lungs.

"All of this is my fault," he whispered again, words muffled by tears. "If I just waited, if I kept you at a distance, if I would take a moment to discipline my heart and keep it tightly chained, then you wouldn't be hurt. I wouldn't fear the possibility of waking up to taste the powder of your bones upon my teeth, hoping that you did shoot me like wild game. And therein lies my true curse: how can I *love* you? How can I allow myself to harbor affections for you when it is your very company that threatens to undo the chains forged for me? How can I protect you when it's me that I am protecting you the most from?"

Love.

Even if she wished to, Jane couldn't muster movement in her muscles. To comfort him, to stand and walk away, anything…

Love. She didn't know what to make of the word, especially when it came from his mouth, the very same one that'd nearly torn her apart, and she knew not if what he had felt in the first place was love at all or some other emotion misinterpreted out of naivety after a lifetime of little companionship. She was certain she didn't love him back—she, in this moment, was terrified to. How could she love something that terrified her as much as he, quietly, captivated her; she hated herself for suddenly finding a muted excitement in being allured by something that held such danger. No wonder she mewled the way she did beneath the Terence-beast's mouth. After all, has already tasted her blood, a part of her within him forever, it may as well have been a marital bond.

But she hoped she could learn to nurture the fondness that'd existed for him to flourish into the very thing she envied her parents for possessing. A love equal parts conditional and unconditional, requited and unrequited.

She sighed and stood, but then shifted so that she sat in his lap, and reached to cradle his face between her palms.

The hazel-brown of his eyes were deep, dark puddles overflowed with utter misery, and she failed to see any semblance of the beast within them. She brushed stray hair from his face, tucking them back into place in a petting motion so that she could see *him*—his vulnerability, his pain for *her*—laid bare and aching.

For her.

Even if it weren't love she yet felt, she knew she *needed* him. Monster and all.

"I can protect myself just fine," Jane whispered despite the ache in her leg, and kissed him.

Her heart sparked, thrilled, when he froze beneath her, held captive under the claiming weight of her mouth. But, after a long moment, his arms wrapped around her and he kissed her back. The hesitation that made his lips feather-light seemed to dissipate as he was overcome with a newfound hunger, desperate to devour his fill, and a growling moan rumbled in the back of his throat as he took Jane's mouth for his own. She held him closer, running her hands through his hair to keep him pressed against her neck even when he went to take a breath. The friction as she ground against his thigh in a needy rut caused stars to dance behind her eyes.

His kisses against the column of her throat were devastatingly tender, his trembling lips becoming like the mouth of the beast, holding her limply between its teeth. Only this time, he didn't dare break her skin and only used such monstrousness to protect her and make himself hers.

"Jane..." he whimpered against her mouth before kissing her again; his breath hitched upon snagging her bottom lip between his teeth. He sighed and nestled into the crook of her neck, nose nuzzling just behind her ear.

Her chest heaved as he pulled her closer into him, and the heat from their bodies being so pressed together lured the thread of a groan from between her breasts. She only dared to open her eyes when she'd grown too afraid that the nightmare beast embraced her, with peeling flesh and bleeding claws, and released a heady breath when she saw it was only Terence—*her* Terence—who held her so passionately.

"I'm a monster, and I do not wish to be..." Terence kissed the very drum of her pulse as she leaned her head back to offer him better access. Tears heated the touch of his mouth, the ghost of another sigh against her skin. "But—*please*—if I'm to be one, then let me be *yours*."

Jane held him there, her fingers curved into hooks of propriety that secured him in place to continue caressing the breathless whispering of her name across her skin. As the tingling, raw heat grew too fierce, she made him pause when she brought her forehead to rest against his. He would devour her later, in one way or another.

Her breaths shallow, she feathered her thumb over his lips

before kissing them again the moment she imagined the beast's teeth hiding behind them, painted red with her blood.

"I will protect you," she whispered in a ragged breath as she pulled away. She licked her lips, savoring the taste of his sadness. "I will protect us. But first, I... I need to show you something."

Eighteen

Jane abandoned Terence in the sitting room, but only for a moment, when she trotted to the conservatory, kicked aside the rug, and removed the loose floorboard to retrieve the moldy little book inside.

When she returned with the book held out before her, Terence remained at the harpsichord, head bent low as he gingerly rubbed fingers over his lips, pink and swollen like a virgin after her first kiss. His brow furrowed as he regarded the book.

"What's this?" he asked as he took it. He leafed through it, and Jane's head throbbed as she tried to focus on what was written inside. An ache of sleeplessness.

"I was hoping you would tell me." With a huff, she stormed over to the windows and closed the curtains, dousing the room in a soft darkness to nurse her headache. Rain and the echo of thunder continued to drone outside. She took the lamp from the desk, lit it, and brought it over to the harpsichord.

"At first, I found these carvings under the guest room bed. I thought I could pass the time deciphering their meanings from your grandfather's books when I happened across *this* one in the conservatory," she explained as she leaned against the instrument. "I found the most peculiar drawings within it, it almost reminded me of a manual a hunter may keep. It's the only book I've seen that could even hint at the beast's machinations. I'd like to know if anything in this book holds any meaning to you so that maybe I could better understand the beast—" *and even you,* "perhaps learn of some of its weaknesses—"

"It's written by my grandfather," Terence whispered, then tapped on a name scrawled inside the front cover.

George Frances Hayes
Sept 1823 — Oct 1895

Terence thumbed through the pages again, and over and over again Jane saw the drawings of the beast and Old Man Hayes' protective wards, blotches of darkness drawn so fiercely they tore through several pages with a single scribble.

At the beginning of the book, there was only one drawing, then there were two several pages later, then three, then four, then three once more. Each drawing correlated with the number of beasts occupying the Hayes family, marking each birth and loss in his own morbid way, Jane supposed.

Terence turned back to the book's beginning, to the very first sketch of the beast, and read the text around it. The handwriting was poor and hastily written.

Today, I stand at the threshold of Heaven. But before I can step across, I must confess to a great sin I have committed: I—George Hayes—have sold my son's soul, and the fate of my lineage, to the Devil, and I am ashamed.

The money was gone. Invested in failed coal mines to the south—damn them. Gambled away out of mad desperation to win back what had been lost. I did not know what else to do, with a young wife and an even younger son to tend to.

It was while Beatrice and I were on holiday to witness the Great Exhibition in London when we came across a rather mystifying group that labeled themselves as "Spiritualists"—so-called vessels that communicated with the spirits that lay beyond the veil.

The Exhibition was meant to only be like a fair, so that we may gawk and awe at manmade wonders amidst our misery. Young and old, rich and poor were united then. I didn't know with who I belonged until we came across a wooden stall on the lawn of Hyde Park. It was draped in burgundy tarps embroidered with symbols of the arcane: elaborate crescent moons, butterflies, eyes, hexafoils, pentagrams. Those operating the stall, selling books and words, wore similar shades of black and burgundy and purple.

The Spiritualists' leader had been a woman of whom I cannot remember the name (had it been 'Florence'? 'Laura'? Perhaps she had been utterly nameless to begin with!) nor can I recall the shapes of her body, though I can recall how she flourished her close connections with Georgiana Houghton like a metal of wartime honor. It was her who, after we sat for tea and told her of our plight, wearily advised us to seek the guidance of spirits of wealth to recover what had been lost. However, she insisted that the work of a Spiritualist was to comfort, both those of the dead and the living, not to ask favors.

Beatrice only thought of them as cons, caught up in the craze of ghostly parlor tricks and seances. She pleaded with me to craft our happiness from what we had. But what happiness could have been forged whilst the impending threat of workhouses loomed across our shoulders?

What more would I have to lose upon pleading to spirits?

I did not know who I prayed to or who I had intended to summon, but I had taken the Spiritualists' book of occult incantations, a page dedicated to subjects of wealth and fortune, and I took to the front room to scribble those arcane symbols and circles, lit candles where instructed, and offered a bowl of chicken's blood in the pentagram's center (though, I must have it be known that the incantation requested blood of a stallion—a luxury too expensive for my pocketbook; I'm certain that if I instead killed a horse the being that haunts this family would be more benign.); then, I began to hum the spell written for me.

At first, it seemed that no one heard me. I felt defeated, fearing that we would remain destitute and unfortunate.

That was until I saw it standing in the middle of the room, in the center of the symbols I'd written in chalk upon the floor, with its feet dipped in the bowl of blood, having risen from the blood, crafted by the blood.

The figure was masculine, finely-sculpted and decorated with piercings of pure gold. Its deformed visage was hidden beneath a fine burgundy veil. Sores and fleshless burns wept blood and gold across its body. From beneath its veil glowed yellow eyes.

Claunek was its name. It said it could provide the wealth I so desperately sought, in a voice that bubbled like honey, and it asked me for a price. And so I named it, enough money to rebuild our home anew and away from the marshes and to have enough money in our pockets so that they were always heavy. And the moment we shook hands, with the palm of my right hand flayed open to complete our deal, a horrific howl tore through the dead of night. The sound of my son, dear little Georgie, being torn apart in order to reshape in the image of Claunek, the newfound god of our wealth. It made him into a beast.

Through its veil, the demon smiled with teeth of gold. Just as it had given wealth, it took a fraction of ours as a price. The male blood in our family had thus been cursed—starting with Georgie, then his eldest son Matthew, then Elias, and finally Terence; their sister Esme, my sole granddaughter, had been spared of the curse, but not the dangers of her brothers' violence. The poor lamb was only eleven.

(Why the boys? I supposed the demon sensed the innate instinct for violence born in the blood of boys and men.)

By day the boys were just that: boys, that may run and play and enjoy the wealth of their family without a care in the world, but by night they are but servants of Clauneck, wearing its skin and forced to crawl on their bellies to commit whatever evils it may not be able to whilst trapped in Hell; it watches over us now from the sitting room mantle, through the eyes of the totem it molded in its image, a reminder of the domain it has crafted for itself here, reeking of brimstone and the dead.

Again and again, the cycle repeats.

I'd been spared their fate, for what reason I do not know, nor can I decide if I'm grateful or ashamed for my lack of beastliness. But I suppose my own beastly nature lies in how I failed to feel sympathy towards the plight of my bloodline, my own greed—my need for more, more, more. But pain could always be cushioned by money; secrets can always be locked away in cellars until they're proper enough to emerge once more; demons can be kept away by the wards of the Spiritualists' books.

Never have I spoken of this to anyone; this book serves as a confession to the sin that I have committed, though I cannot say that I seek forgiveness from anyone other than God and His angels—

Terence threw the book down as he turned to a page with several drawings of the beast. The demon Claunek was scribbled in as well, its name stuffing the margins. Jane recognized the crude drawings of that skinless face. It was what taunted her in that nightmare organ-room—the idol atop the fireplace, leering down at them, silently giggling. Old Man Hayes' drawing failed to capture the rot of the demon's boiled skin, the way its eyes hung from its sockets, the stench of Hell it carried with it.

Jane flinched as Terence pushed the stool out from beneath him and stormed across the room to the bookshelf. He took hold of the family photograph, grip tight as he scowled down at it. Tears mottled his face, red as wrath.

Jane came up behind him, though kept her distance as she watched his back. Old Man Hayes sat too calmly in the portrait's center. The blurred eyes, seeking out the demon haunting them; the burned hand a mark of their deal, in the name of regaining wealth lost. Looming behind them were those misshapen shadows, heads elongated and ears pointed. Perhaps those weren't the shadows of setpieces, but rather the echoes of the beasts within them, servants of Claunek.

A crack spiderwebbed across the glass.

"My sister was murdered," Terence started, strained. He sneered, and Jane saw vestiges of the beast in the fury etched into his profile. "My mother wasted away, my brothers and father reside in unmarked graves. My life has been torment, because of *him*. It was no wonder he never wanted to see us: the bastard was too much of a coward to face his victims."

He snarled and threw the photo to the ground, and glass splintered everywhere. Jane covered her face in an instinctive jolt and hopped back with a small yelp.

"Terence..." She started as he stared down at his mess with ragged pants.

He didn't seem to hear her.

"And then *you*—" he jabbed a shaking finger at the idol atop the mantle.

Claunek.

Terence looked as though he were trying to form words, lips trembling and eyes transfixed, but none came out. His mouth peeled back to flash his teeth in a wolf-ish sneer. He charged to the fireplace and viciously snatched up the idol. He clutched it in a fist. Its eyes seemed to glow from beneath its veil, a wordless dare.

It was as though he had many things to say and they were all wrestling to come out at once. What *was* one to say when they cradled their creator and eternal tormentor in the palm of their hand?

"You... You did this," he coughed out. His body shivered, and a vein throbbed at his temple, with restraint. "And I banish you back to Hell—" He raised a hand to throw it to the ground, just as he did the portrait, but the action was abruptly cut short.

He suddenly doubled over with a violent retching sound. Each heave lurched him closer to the floor. The idol fell heavily from his grasp into the carpet. It stared at them both with its gleaming eyes.

Terence clutched his throat as he continued to gag, as if Claunek reached its unseen hands outwards to strangle him. The dim shadows he cast across the curtains, hunchbacked and feral, resembled too closely a wolf.

Jane rushed to his side and, unsure of whether to grab him or smack his back to loosen whatever may be clogged in his throat, she elected to gingerly grab his shoulders and give him a blunt shake.

"Terence, what—"

His head snapped to her, and Jane reeled backward with a gasp as he looked at her with yellow eyes. Not golden, *yellow*. The color of illness and Hell. The eyes of the beast. Blood had begun to ooze from corners where flesh tightened and pulled taut.

Blood foamed from his mouth as he gurgled out something resembling words. Eventually, she was able to make out only two: "C-curtains... *Jane!*"

Jane paused as her blood suddenly ran cold.

The curtains.

She rushed to the windows and threw aside the accursed fabric, and was met with her horrified reflection in a darkened window, the world outside having fallen into a rain-bloated darkness. It was night. The time for the beast and Claunek to roam.

Jane's ribs rattled with a wheeze as Terence choked on another harsh gag, this one so violent it threw him to his knees.

Another retch shook his body when his pestilence-yellow eyes sought her.

Jane's skin crawled, almost in the same manner in which the flesh of his throat twitched. It seemed as though something was wriggling its way upwards from deep within. Skin strained and split, and blood wept from the opened seams. Just as wiry fur sprouted from the wounds in hellish splinters, Terence's crooked hands clutched at his neck, fluids and viscera leaking from between his fingers, his eyes, his mouth—everywhere.

His beastly eyes found Jane once more, and they *begged.*

Help, save me, end me—run.

All Jane could do was cower in his chair, curling deeper into herself in an attempt to hide from the horror bleeding before her.

She screamed.

A muzzle burst forth from his mouth, cutting off his howl and sending a shower of teeth and blood to make way for a maw that craved sin. Chunks of a mandible hung from between snarling fangs in gelatinous strings.

The skin continued to unzip down his throat, revealing the gray mane clumped together by globs of blood, as he staggered to his feet.

He lurched forward with a harsh cough and crashed against the harpsichord. The veins of the hands gripping the instrument wriggled until nails gave way to claws that splintered into the dark wood. He started to stumble toward the hallway on contorting limbs that were betraying him. Left in his wake, all the way to the entrance hall, was a trail of dripping blood and stripped flesh, and Jane watched him from the window as he threw himself into the rain-slick yard where he continued to writhe and scream.

Each flash of lightning revealed a new stage of the metamorphosis, a new abomination, as the beast unfurled from his back. It tore itself free from the confines of mortal flesh until all that remained of Terence was a puddle of gore the beast howled over.

Its throat rumbled as it bent forward to lap up its discarded pelt of man with a steaming tongue.

Before she could distract it from its morsel, Jane rushed to slam the front door shut, then she turned to retrieve the pin-knife from the guest room. Every one of her stilted footfalls was accompanied by a beastly howl outside, a demonic giggle within and beneath the floorboards.

The blade pierced her palm when she blindly grabbed it from between the folds of the ruined quilts and droplets of blood spotted the hem of her dress as she returned to the sitting room. She was careful to step around the lost pieces of flesh and shards of bone-turned-cartilage.

Claunek's doll still lay crookedly on the floor, amidst the blood and shattered glass. It was snickering, silently, she just knew it.

She sneered at the thing. All she could imagine was the demon from her nightmare, with its flayed face and bulging eyes that leaked golden tears, standing before Terence's grandfather as he bartered away the humanity of his son and forthcoming generations in exchange for petty wealth. She imagined the demon haunting the house, watching over boys becoming beasts, shedding their skins every night and every morning, with a smile upon its inhuman lips.

She imagined that Claunek had been *there* when she first entered the house, introducing itself to her without her knowing when she'd brushed against it. It was a faint touch, but enough to have the demon set its sights on her and send its beast to investigate this stranger in its domain. She grabbed the idol and gave it a squeeze. Had her blood upon the beast's tongue deepened her connection with Claunek? Was the beast's bloodlust its own desire or the demon's orchestration?

She didn't know, nor did she care, as either way meant death for her. She had grown exhausted of demons and beasts, and their games.

A scream split the air around Jane, shrill and sending a chill through her blood. The stank of burning flesh curdled in her nose. Smoke rose from the idol where the knife seared deeper into its golden visage. Jane did nothing to stop the screaming or the burning of gold. All she could feel was a morbid awe—and triumph.

Silver.

Was the beast's aversion to it an extension of the demon's own weaknesses?

Only one way to find out.

Without a second thought, Jane knelt atop the idol and plunged the knife into it. It was unlike stabbing metal or even wood, but rather like stabbing the mud-like flesh of the beast in Matthew's grave: slick and slimy, and from the wounds flowed forth blood and gold. She felt as though she were cutting through burnt flesh, peeling it aside and revealing something raw and bleeding beneath.

The house shook beneath a violent keening from outside. Stronger than thunder, and filled with an ire that belonged not in nature.

She didn't stop her assault on the idol until the house itself seemed to scream. And everything fell deathly still as she plunged the pin into its eyes. Outside, the beast was howling, anguished and starving for vengeance.

The beast would be coming for her, she knew it. She harmed its unholy master. She would need to hunt it before it could hunt her.

Keeping the pin-knife in a fist slick with red and golden fluid, she took the Winchester propped against the fireplace in the other.

But what was she to do once this beast was hunted? Would she be able to somehow rescue Terence from within it, somehow? She thought of the beast in the grave that seemed to have been wearing two skins, Terence shedding flesh to become monstrous, even his nightmare visage that appeared to her flayed itself during its pleasures.

Jane swallowed thickly. Could his salvation—and even her own—lie in her skinning a beast birthed from hell?

Once more, she mused, "Only one way to find out."

At the front door, she slipped into her coat, stuffed the remaining ammunition into the Winchester, tightened her grip on the knife to assure herself of its presence, took hold of her parasol, steeled her nerves, and stepped out into the downpour.

Nineteen

HEN SHE DIDN'T IMMEDIATELY SPOT THE BEAST, searching desperately for the glow of its eyes or the flash of its fangs, Jane opened her mouth and screamed into the darkness. She bared her teeth and howled again, calling for the beast so that it could come to her.

"I'm here, you mongrel! Come at me! Eat me!"

Mud slurped around her boots and parasol, but she persevered as she marched deeper and deeper into the yard; through the rain and thunder, she thought she heard a sound that could've been Mrs. Foster calling for her from the house, but she ignored it.

Especially once she heard the grunting of something rushing through the reeds, coming right toward her. The beast's hulking shadow seemed to swallow the night around it, making it an all-consuming void with its eyes—and teeth—trained on her.

It *knew*. She had undone its maker, and now she was to undo *it*, too.

Jane raised the rifle, butt pressing into her still-aching shoulder. She tried to stay her hand, to train her mark on the beast, but the rain, adrenaline shaking through her, and bleariness that'd otherwise be cured by her spectacles made it near impossible. At last, she fired. The shot either grazed the beast or startled it because it swerved with a fierce wine, striking her with its passing body.

She fell back with a yelp, having tripped over one of the cemetery's headstones. The gun was flung skywards until it was caught in one of the angels' outstretched arms and the remaining ammunition was scattered in the mud.

She hardly had any time to regain her bearings, a grip now secure on the knife in her pocket, before she heard the skidding of paws through mud as the beast turned to rush her like a bull with its eyes set on murder. The cemetery's angels watched over them, anticipation creaking through their rain-slick wings.

In one hand she grasped the knife and in the other, she clutched the parasol.

Come at me! Come, boy, come on! Finish what you started!

As the beast charged her once again, she staggered back to her feet and raised both weapons with a yell.

She thrust the parasol forward, and her screams stuttered when it was met with a force and a horrible, wet squelching as the parasol lodged itself securely in the back of the beast's throat.

The beast choked on the blood that began to bubble at the corners of its maw. Blood showered as it yanked away from Jane and viciously shook its head in an attempt to dislodge the parasol. Its retching became growls of frustration as it continued to choke, and she took the opportunity to attack.

She screamed and charged at it. She tackled it into the mud and plunged the knife into its neck. It brayed a horrible scream when flesh sizzled and a fountain of blood steamed beneath her palm.

The beast arched its neck in an attempt to bite her, seemingly forgetting that it still had an object jammed in its mouth that'd hinder such an action. It tried shaking her off when biting proved to be useless.

Jane retaliated by stabbing again—and then again, and again, deeper and deeper each time she brought the knife down until she was more soaked in steaming blood than rain. Wafting off the both of them was the smoke of hellfire from which its forefather spawned.

The beast swayed on its feet, but that didn't stop Jane from stabbing its torso, dragging away strips of loosened flesh that bubbled and seeped into the dirt once they hit the ground.

Heaving, the beast collapsed, perhaps from its loss of blood, asphyxiation, Jane's assault, or some culmination of the three. Jane thought—*feared*—it died for a moment until she saw its sides shudder beneath a fading breath.

Now to see if he can be freed...

After hesitating for half a moment, she plunged her knife into the center of the beast's chest and sawed through the skin as though dressing a deer. It was an action she had witnessed her father do several times, and the muscles in her hands did all they could to muster those memories whenever they weren't acutely aware of the foreign meat caking every inch of them.

She pushed until she felt the knife scratch against the bone of the beast's sternum (*Please, don't let it be Terence's*, she begged, soaked in gore). She dragged the knife all the way down to the pubis, where she started to peel back skin.

Like removing a coat, using the knife to tear away connective sinews, Jane hurried to slough off layers of skin, throwing each piece behind her with a savage grunt, and not even bothering to look as they bubbled and disintegrated. It was different from dressing a deer, but Jane needed to remind herself that this was not a deer. It wasn't even a thing of this realm. There wasn't even a muscle layer to peel away from, no orange jelly of subcutaneous fatty tissues, no tendons to snap. There was hardly even any bone to cut around, just flimsy infrastructure built with a firm gel-like cartilage that gave away beneath her clawing fingers. It was layers upon layers of slop, like a rotted onion. She sawed away until she found the paleness of human flesh, warm to the touch, spasming beneath her fingertips.

Terence.

It inspired fervor that jerked through her limbs as they continued the labor of shucking away more layers of beast to uncover the man beneath.

Too slowly, the beast's choking roars dulled into pathetic whimpers, and then utter silence when Jane took hold of its mane in both her hands, and yanked it away. It detached with little resistance, as though peeling away an old strip of adhesive, but with the mane came the beast's head, whole and still choking on the parasol. Staggering beneath its weight, she heaved it aside with a grunt.

Its tongue lolled out of an agape maw, and its eyes, lifeless and unfocused, still, somehow, managed to peer up at her. Or perhaps it was Claunek itself watching her. Scorning her victory and quirking the dead beast's lips in the faintest of smiles, wishing her a begrudging congratulations she earned with blood, before the thing began to melt.

The pelt oozed and steamed, deflating into putty. Pieces soaked into the mud, drawn back to Hell where they never should have left in the first place.

And Jane roared at the puddle. She bared her teeth and screamed until the eyes were completely gone, bursting into yellow gunk with a *pop* and puff of steam. The earthy taste of blood soaked her tongue and the back of her throat.

Once the breath had gone from her lungs, unable to scream anymore even if she wanted to, she turned to look at the naked man still curled in the dirt. Rain was washing the gore from his body.

Jane rushed over to him and slapped away whatever remained of the beast's entrails. Tiny cuts from where the knife nicked him bled gently, the blood red and not smoldering. Not the blood of the beast or Claunek.

His.

She hauled him into her lap and patted his cheeks, calling his name. His face was slack but his brow was drawn tightly together, as though he were trapped in the throes of a bad dream. She wanted to wake him up if it meant scaring that nightmare away.

She begun to fear that her parasol had skewered too deep and penetrated him, too, but as she started to feel around his body for any other wounds, fingers ghosting over the chaffed scars of his throat and wrists, he gasped violently, eyes snapping open as his lungs swallowed a desperate breath of air.

It startled Jane at first, but then she captured his face in her hands, pleading for his eyes to meet hers. Her thumbs rubbed over his lips, peeling them back just enough to show that his teeth were, blessedly, blunt and human.

But he didn't look at her. He instead gawked at the sky above. He didn't even blink as the rain splattered across his face.

"W-We... We are outside?" he rasped, throat bobbing in harsh a swallow.

For some reason she couldn't quite place, Jane chuffed out an exasperated laugh. "Yes, quite an astute observation—"

"And it... it is dark. Is it nighttime?" His eyes widened as panic seemingly took hold of him. A hand reached up to take hers that had now rested on his shoulder. His grip turned his knuckles white.

"Well, I was hoping it may be nearly dawn by now—"

"Outside... *at night... Jane*—"

She pressed a palm to his mouth, silencing him.

"Yes, yes, Terence," she breathed. Her eyes blinked rapidly, against the heat of tears and the chill of rain. "We are outside."

He continued to urgently search the sky, perhaps for an answer, or something to calm himself, but after a long time, as the rain began to quiet, his eyes finally flittered to look up at Jane. A hand, still slick with the beast's meaty bits, reached up to skim across her cheek. It left a streak of brown gore in its wake. Jane already felt it seeping deep into her skin, but she couldn't bring herself to care.

His brows furrowed as he brushed her face again, perhaps convinced that what he was living now wasn't reality at all, but instead a nightmare.

Jane huffed out another small laugh, tears now in her eyes as she leaned into his touch, using her hand to keep it there, and she briefly kissed his knuckles. He was alive—that much she could celebrate, at least, even if there was the chance that it may have been minute and pointless.

"Jane..." Terence started, but Jane silenced him with another kiss, gentle, chaste, cherishing. She didn't care that he tasted of mud, blood, and brimstone, for he also tasted of freedom.

Twenty

OLLOWING A DAY OF UNEASY QUIET, EVERYONE seemingly too apprehensive to speak on what just transpired the night before, Terence insisted that he stay in the cellar as evening began to fall upon the Drowning House. As much as Jane wished to plead with him to stay with her upstairs and to join her in her hopes that she, somehow, slain the beast, banished Claunek, and freed him of whatever curse that had been put upon him, she let him go down to the cellar with a heavy heart and bated breath. She then went up to the washroom, locking it behind her.

Instead of going to bed, Jane huddled herself in the tub stuffed with quilts and a throw pillow. She hugged her knees to her chest and held her breath as she waited. She listened for any sort of screams or roars or the clanking of chains. But as none of those came, the creeping silence made her afraid. Perhaps something worse had come to happen.

What if Claunek had clawed its way up from Hell to possess Terence itself? Would it find a way to turn perhaps a Wolf's Run villager into another one of its beasts to hunt them down out of revenge?

She shuddered and resisted the urge to vomit. She'd lost the knife in the marsh, and the Winchester, likely now clogged with mud, still rested in the stone angel's arms. She'd no defenses left.

A week ago, Jane wouldn't ever have entertained the idea of such a thing happening, for demons weren't real to her and subjects of the occult were merely party tricks. She firmly believed in science, not magic! But now, the idea made her feel sick. Magic, in some form, did exist. And she would be content if she never even heard a murmuring of it ever again.

She didn't know how much time passed before the silence became unbearable and she hauled herself from the tub. She tiptoed down the stairs, each step as tentative as the last; she feared that a sound as simple as a creaking floorboard could trigger some sort of horrific event. But as she reached the bottom of the steps, she paused to listen, and, upon hearing no disconcerting sounds nor encountering any beast or demon, she hesitantly released a breath through her lips.

But when she stepped into the sitting room and saw Terence looming at the windows, she practically leaped out of her skin with a yelp. Her cry startled him as well and he whirled around to meet her.

He stared at her with that dazed expression again, as if he were looking upon a dream rather than something of flesh and blood. He wore only a robe, the front of which opened to expose a triangle of bare chest and the pink slant of his throat's scar. His hair came to possess some semblance of grooming, his face clean, his form silhouetted by a hazy silver light filtering in through the windows. Shadows deepened the hollows of his face, his cheeks, his eyes, and starlight highlighted the silver at his temples.

Jane couldn't help but find the scene utterly attractive, nearly romantic, in its own sort of way—though she couldn't decide if it was because of how... lasciviously he was dressed or if it was the fact she was seeing *him* standing here rather than a beast ready to pounce on her to tear her to shreds.

His mouth nearly toyed into a smile, eyes glittering briefly, but then a worried pinch creased their corners as his lips fell slack.

"What time of day is it, Jane?" He whispered, hoarse. "Is it still nighttime?"

"Yes," she said. "Shouldn't be any later than nine, I reckon."

Too eagerly, she joined him by the open window. A gust of cool air—as well as her own nerves and selfish cravings—pressed her against him.

The sky was utterly clear. No clouds, no rain. Jane wanted to cry.

Stars speckled the velvet dark that caressed a low-hanging crescent moon, beaming down at them with a gentle smile. The smell of rain permeated the room, and Jane's nose scrunched slightly when she could still smell the acrid stank of the beast's discarded pelt.

"*Stars*, Jane..." she jumped when his breath disturbed the hair beside her ear. When she looked up at him, she saw him staring into the night sky, eyes twinkling with tears—starlight of their own. When one of those tears slipped down his cheek, she reached up to catch it with her fingertip. "I've never seen stars before... Have they always been this wonderful?"

Jane didn't look at the stars. She had seen them all her life, and no longer did they hold whimsy for her. Instead, she was captivated by his wonder, enthralled by a man denied a pleasure as simple as looking into the night sky, and her pride coaxed her to smile. It was a sad, soft grin, but a smile nonetheless. She was the one who had given him the stars and the moon.

She sighed and rested her head against his shoulder as she looked out the window, deep into the marsh's still waters reflecting the moonlight. She wondered if the beast lavished under such moonlight, so that Terence could have tasted some kind of nightly beauty in some way.

"No," she said at last.

She turned to cup his face. His eyes—his *blessed*, human eyes—continued their glittering as her thumbs ran the lengths of his cheeks. A gentle sigh rushed from his nose as he closed those eyes and pressed into her touch.

Such a good boy...

She craned her neck to kiss his human mouth where she whispered against human skin, "They've only become wonderful since you've looked at them."

Epilogue

BY THE MORNING OF THE FOLLOWING SECOND DAY, THE
marshes had drained enough for Ruben to take a bicycle to
Wolf's Run so that he could call for a carriage for the rest of them.

Jane could barely contain her excitement, and fear, at being
able to leave this wretched house. She paced the entryway, bag and
ruined parasol in hand.

Mrs. Foster had the dress she first wore to the Drowning
House cleaned and pressed, and at last Jane finally felt right to be
wearing her proper pelt again. Almost. Her face was still naked,
stripped bare of her makeup. It was ruined by bruises and scrapes,
and a nasty scratch trailing from her bottom lip to chin that would
certainly leave a scar.

All she could think about, after a time, was what her mother
would be like upon her return. Would she be frantic? Would she be
understanding? Or would she just be working on her watercolors

again as if Jane never left in the first place? Jane at least knew she'd panic over her injury and the stilted stride Jane now walked with. Mrs. Sterling would first fret over Jane's well-being, as all good mothers do, but would then bemoan the grace in Jane's stride becoming permanently interrupted rather than the fact that her daughter had been mauled.

Thinking about the wound made it ache suddenly, the pain settling in Jane's knee. She paused her pacing to lift her skirt and look at the bandaged limb. The gauze was marked with the faintest imprints of pink and yellow. Jane had to admit that she, too, feared the scar would be both ugly and damaging to her stride. At the same time, smug pride flared in her chest. Neither of her sisters, her parents, or anyone else she knew, would bear scars from a battle won against a devil. She had gone to discover her own new beast—her own *Ichthyosaur*—and all she would be able to show for it were a few scars and a new companion.

At least the beast spared my face... somewhat.

"What were you going to tell your mother?" Terence's voice startled Jane as he plodded down the stairs. He wore a fine green vest, which stood out brightly against the black of his tweed overcoat. His face was smooth from a fresh shave; Jane smiled with approval. He held a proper cane—which he used to gesture to her leg and then offered to her.

She took the cane, rolled it in her hands, and wrinkled her nose at it. It was a simple wooden one. Finely made, yes, but still plain. She decided to hold onto it, but she preferred to lean on her, admittedly, more fashionable parasol, even though it was stained with mud and blood.

"I do not know," she said and dropped her skirt. "Haven't decided. Perhaps I will say that we had a run-in with a dog—but that I won and that the dog is worse for wear."

That rose a wry chuckle from Terence as he joined her in the entryway, "You wouldn't be wholly wrong in that statement."

The space was quiet, stiff, between them for a moment before he cleared his throat. He wrung a pair of smart gloves and a scarlet scarf between his hands.

"I've... never had a chance to properly thank you, Jane—and to apologize."

"For?" Jane knew damn well what for, but she wanted to hear him say it. She smiled expectantly.

Her smile fell, though, when he looked at her. The earnestness in his gaze tamed her need to be playful.

"You freed me," he whispered. "And I don't think I'll ever find a way to forgive myself that it was at the cost of your own blood but... thank you, Jane."

Yes, I know. I gave you the stars. Now say it again... Please.

When he didn't, she rolled her shoulders in a masculine shrug. "I'm an American. It's practically instinct for me to viciously dress a thing I've put a bullet in."

His laugh was muted, and Jane's giggle faltered when he took her face in his hands. The calluses were tender against her cheeks and she savored their heat with a hungry sigh.

"Thank you, Jane," he whispered, lower now, and his breath brushed against her mouth. "I fear that I shall forever dread the setting sun. I've always dreamt of what music was made by crickets and bats and reeds kissed by the shifting winds, and perhaps one day I may come to cherish their song as a herald of freedom, just as I do dawn's first songbirds. But I hope I may grow to find excitement in finally looking upon the night sky to see the moon and stars I've only ever heard tales of." Their lips brushed, though only briefly, before he whispered, "Only if you'll join me, and teach me to appreciate their wonder."

Teach me.

A command of his own that threaded its way through her ribs and the valves of her heart. She supposed that there was now much for him to learn, no longer bound by a beast in his blood but rather the scars of manhood.

She took hold of his chin and rubbed her thumb over the dimple there before leaning up to press into him with a kiss.

She wondered if this was another piece of Claunek's torture: leaving bones haunted and souls scarred. Terence could unlearn that pain inflicted upon the boys of the Hayes bloodline. And he would have to do it on his own, as it was a curse that could only be broken in time. Jane could offer a hand to guide and support him, though the path toward healing was a quest for him alone to embark on; to complete a quest of betterment would truly set him further apart from his fellow men.

On the other side of the door was the telltale slosh of mud churned by hooves and wheels, followed by disgruntled blows of horses made to trudge through dirty roads.

Jane ran a hand down the lapel of his coat as she took a step back. "It is a shame your fossils were ruined. They were rather unique finds... I think?"

He laughed, a hearty, rolling sound, and the corners of his eyes pinched pleasantly.

"Jane Sterling, I love you," his chuckle, as sheepish as it was, inspired her skin to prickle with gooseflesh as he leaned to her ear, "And if you'll allow me, in time, I would be honored to clean away my sins from your skin beneath my tongue."

Before she could admonish him with a smack (or a kiss), she squealed beneath the nibbling peck he left on her cheek, and he left her to go out and greet their vehicle to a new life. Her heart stuttered and her face went hot, but she couldn't help but grin.

She watched him slide through the mud as he crossed the yard to greet Ruben driving a wagon pulled by two draft horses, his shoulders held back and teeth flashed in a smile, with a revitalized confidence. The confidence of a man unbound.

I suppose I may come to love you, too, Terence Hayes.

Jane smiled as she leaned against the doorway to give her leg a rest. She watched him through the gentle mist before she sighed and pushed herself off to join them. Ms. Hudson and Mrs. Foster came close behind her, swaddled in cloaks and with purses clutched in their twiddling hands. Mrs. Foster, without stopping her conversation with Ms. Hudson, gave Jane a knowing look. Though it'd seemed to be a wordless rule to not further ask about the beast, or rather the sudden lack thereof, out of a fear that their foolish hopes would somehow summon the beast right back, Mrs. Foster in her silence still seemed to know... The beast, the evil, was now gone. They were *all* free.

Jane held her chin higher. If they'd been so quick to herald her an executioner by bringing them to the house, then perhaps now they could see her as a savior.

Wound around Jane's heels in ribboning whisps, as she let Terence hoist her into the wagon after stealing another kiss, were the echoes of the screams of beasts and demons she had slain. She bit her lip against a rising smile.

Acknowledgments

I DO NOW KNOW WHERE TO START OR WHO TO ALL THANK for all the time, love, energy, and support that went into making this daydream into a reality. To start: thank you, Mom and Dad, for *everything*—and for letting me grow up consuming copious amounts of 80s and 90s media. Love you, guys!

Thank you to Maggie for being one of the first soundboards for me to ramble about ideas to and your continuous support of our weird little WIPs; thank you Dorian for the kind words said about this book and its characters, and having the chance to chat about books, publishing, and doomed arctic expeditions with you; thank you both for being some of the biggest, most vocal cheerleaders for this book when it was still an ugly brain child and for helping me realize this book could be something great.

Thank you to the beta readers who helped me hone the identity of this book and for being some of the first eyes to read it.

Thank you to the artists who made this book more beautiful than I ever could have imagined: Erika, for the cover of my dreams, and Mariska, for interior illustrations that truly encapsulate the atmosphere of this novel.

Thank you to the readers who gave this book, and me, a chance. And thank you to my sisters: Hailey, for being a source of inspiration for Jane's dramatics, and Olivia, for being one of those readers to read the manuscript I emailed you, and not even 10 minutes later looked me in the eye and asked me, "Do they *really* end up together?"

About The Author

JOSEPHINE TAYLOR IS A NEWS EDITOR BY DAY AND A WRITER by night. Whenever she isn't writing, she can be found haunting the local library, going on long car rides, collecting garden gnomes and vintage clinch cover books, and cuddling with her fur children, which consist of two guinea pigs, Peach and Daisy, and a cat, Sammie. She currently lives in the Wisconsin Northwoods in the company of Hodags and other forest beasts.

The Bones We Haunt is her debut novel.

Let's Connect!

Author website | josephinetaylorbooks.weebly.com
Email | josephinetaylorauthor@gmail.com
Instagram | jo.taylor.books
Twitter | JoTaylorBooks
Bluesky | jojopenguinwrites.bsky.social
Tumblr | theboarsbride
TikTok | jo.taylor.books

www.ingramcontent.com/pod-product-compliance
Lightning Source LLC
Chambersburg PA
CBHW061218170626

46809CB00007B/2522